Duct Tape & Cheeseburgers

80+ Jokes & Stories guaranteed to redden your tomatoes & split your buns

By: Kenneth D. Simpson

With Contributions From
Fred the Fish
George the Gator
Helga the Russian
Zedd the Zebra
Tony the Banjo-Playing Tyrannosaurus Rex

As well as

Joyce "Close That Fridge Door" Platz
Bill "Selective Hearing" Platz
Tammy "Greased Lightning" Cole
Lacey "*Onyx Sabre*" Ware
Ari "Hitmonlee" Summit
Alicia "Turbo Waddle" Pretty
Randall "The Reaper" Gibson
Kevin "Morphin' Time" White
Anna "5 o' clock Somewhere" Anderson
Jesse "Missing in Action" Diffee
Timothy "Heavy Machinery" Duty
Samantha "To Japan" Cole
Christina "By Moonlight" Brame
Christina "Captain Planet" Jones
Jason "Grumpy Old Man" Kirby
Jeremy "Dead-Eye" Foulks
Mitchell "The Red Wolf" Blalock
Sharona "The Hufflepuff" Nickerson
Warren "Dumbledore's Army" Huber
Vicky "Mrs. John Wayne" Simpson
Charles "Arkansas Redneck" Simpson
Zack "The Fact" Benham

WARNING

THIS BOOK CONTAINS ADULT-THEMED HUMOR AND WORDS NOT SUITABLE FOR CHILDREN. AS SUCH, THIS BOOK IS NOT SUITABLE FOR ANY PERSONS UNDER THE AGE OF 16.

READER DISCRETION IS ADVISED.

Introduction

Hello there. My name is Kenneth Simpson. For those who don't know me it's of the utmost importance to note that I am (or at least try to be) a funny person. Funny-sounding, funny-looking, funny-smelling—you get the picture.

I want to take just a moment to thank you for taking your time and spending your hard-earned (or ill-gotten, if that is indeed the case, though I'm not one to judge) money to buy this humorous collection that I've spent some significant time (over ten years) assembling.

I will confess that this book represents one of my oldest dreams. You see, I've been writing fiction (both fanfiction and my own original works) since the age of nine, but one book I always wanted to publish was a book of jokes and stories that I'd heard and collected over the years. This dream especially rocketed into the stratosphere once I hit my puberty years and became more privy to the jokes that most adults don't tell their children. At times I wondered if I would ever accomplish it, as my life has been a rollercoaster ride with lows even stronger than the highs.

And yet that's perhaps one of the greatest lessons I've learned, particularly in the weeks leading up to the conclusion and publication of this book. No matter how dark the night gets, regardless of how scary life seems and how hopeless things might feel, that darkness is never complete, not if you can find something—anything—to laugh at. Time doesn't heal all wounds—that's a lie. The fact is some wounds never heal. That's just a fact of life—you better get used to it. But laughter *can* dull the pain and help us move forward, one day at a time. I've always said that if I can make at least one person's day better then *my* day's not wasted.

I also feel like an explanation is in order. This title actually came from a former friend of mine when I was doing security work at a local Nestle plant. I'd been stationed for the day at one of our two truck gates and this friend, our site supervisor, called out to ask if I needed anything. I advised I needed some duct tape to fix some piece of equipment or another, I can't really remember what it was, exactly. I then amended this to add that I could also use a cheeseburger. We then joked that duct tape and cheeseburgers was the story of my life. After all, as a simple country bumpkin, there's little I can't fix with duct tape, and cheeseburgers have always been my favorite food.

Now, as for those first five persons listed on the aforementioned page— they're all me. Well, mostly. Working at the Dollar General in Monette, Arkansas, I would always wear my name tag on a lanyard so that my name was always visible to anyone speaking with me (I hated clipping it to my shirt because it'd always get knocked off). However, there would always be those special people who'd ask me "What's your name, again?" I'd look down at my badge, look them in the face, and then respond "Fred the Fish". Later, my sisters, my friends, and I would jokingly make up George the Gator, Fred's grumpy twin brother, and Zedd the Zebra, their crazy uncle. As for the banjo-playing T-Rex, that's something that's been a regular staple of my dreams for the last sixteen years. Anymore, it's one of the running jokes of my life. As for Helga the Russian—my very best friend, Lacey, often mimics a Russian accent that I have taken to calling Helga.

So, please enjoy the stories and images that follow and again, thank you for giving your time and energy to a crazy nerd's words.

This book is hereafter and forevermore dedicated to those broken souls who get lost in the darkness and never emerge again. To those strong saints in flesh who choose to ignore their own crippling pain so that others might smile and laugh, even as it costs them their lives, we love you, and we salute you. On the other side of darkness may you find the peace you so richly deserve and the rest you so desperately lacked.

General Jokes

A Farmer in Court

A while back an old farmer named Leroy James was transporting a cow from his farm to the fairgrounds when a semi-truck ran a stop sign and hit his trailer. Initially, Leroy refused to file suit against the driver and his company, but as his medical bills mounted he soon found himself left with no other choice but to seek damages against them. Unfortunately, however, he'd drained so much of his money from the bank that he was forced to settle for a public legal advocate. Meanwhile, the truck driver's company had been able to hire themselves the best and fanciest city lawyers that money could buy.

In the courtroom, the company's lawyer immediately went for the throat.

"Mr. James, is it true that when EMS arrived at the scene of the incident—an incident *you* helped cause—you refused medical treatment?"

"Well, yes, it is, but that's only—"

"In fact, were your exact words *not* 'I don't need anything; I'm perfectly fine.'?"

"I only—"

"Mr. James, may I remind you that you *are* under oath?"

"Well, yes, I know that, but—"

"Please just answer the question, Mr. James. Were those or weren't those your words?"

"Yes, sir, I did say that, but only because my prized cow, Bessie—"

"Your honor, I—"

"I only refused medical attention because Bessie—"

"Mr. James, you refused medical attention because you weren't hurt. You've only recently filed suit against my client because your farm is failing, isn't that right?!"

"I *was* hurt!" Leroy argued. "I just refused because Bessie—"

"Your honor, I think we've heard all we need to hear. Clearly this lawsuit is ridiculous. If you could instruct the Plaintiff to answer the question—"

"Young man, if you'd shut up I could explain that it's only because Bessie—"

"Your honor, please instruct the Plaintiff to answer the question."

"Easy there, Mr. Smith." The judge ordered. "It's clear there's something important he wants to tell us about Bessie; I would be most interested in hearing it myself. Mr. James, please continue."

"Well, your honor, after that driver blew past the stop sign he hit me in the trailer so hard that it snapped my seatbelt and sent me out my door. I ended up in a ditch and as I tried collecting myself I could hear Bessie. I could just tell, sir, that she was in some mighty real pain. I tried pulling myself up to the side of the road, you know, so maybe I could get to her and make sure she was alright.

"I made it up to the edge of the ditch but I couldn't stand up. As Bessie continued to moan a state trooper pulled up. He got out of his car and walked over to where Bessie had been spilled out on the other side of the road. He looked at her and then he pulled out his pistol and he shot her! Then he comes over to me, with his gun in his hand, and tells me 'Your cow was in bad shape so I shot her. Now, how are you feeling? Are you okay?' Now tell me, your honor, what the hell would *you* have said?"

Batter Up!

Betty came home late one night after a particularly hard day at the office. She was so tired that she didn't even stop to grab something to eat. Instead, unbuttoning her shirt, she walked upstairs and went right for her bedroom. Given the lateness of the hour she simply knew her husband must already be in bed and fast asleep, so because of this she was quiet and cautious when she opened the door to her bedroom. However, to her surprise the lamp on her bedside table was on. She carefully studied her bed and soon noticed that there were four feet under the blanket instead of just her husband's two. And they were moving

Enraged, Betty strode over to the closet, pulled out her husband's baseball bat, and then returned to her bed where she the then proceeded to begin hitting every inch of the bed as hard as she possibly could, screaming and cursing as she went. Betty didn't stop until neither figure moved.

Once satisfied that her husband and his mistress had been properly punished, she went back downstairs to the kitchen, in desperate need of a drink. However, when she reached the kitchen she was astonished to find the light on and her husband sitting at the dinner table, calmly reading a newspaper.

"Wh—"

"Oh! Hi, Baby, I didn't hear you come in." He greeted, sitting the paper down upon the table. "Listen, before I forget: your parents came down for a surprise visit so I let them have our bedroom. Why don't you go up and say 'hello'?"

Refrigerator to Heaven

Three men approached the Pearly Gates, having just died and passed on. As they reached the gates to Heaven, however, Saint Peter appeared, holding up a hand to check their progress. He explained to the new arrivals that, because Heaven was near-capacity, they just couldn't let all three of them in.

"I want you each to tell me how you died." Saint Peter said. "Because whoever had the worst death gets into Heaven and the other two have to go on to Hell."

The first man steps forward. "Well, Saint Peter, sir, I suspected my wife was having an affair. I didn't want to admit it but lately the evidence has become too obvious to ignore. So the other day I took off early from work to go home and surprise her.

"However, when I arrived I found her in the bedroom wrapped in a towel—but her body was completely dry, so I knew she hadn't just got out of the shower. Angry, I searched the apartment and at last I found a man in his underwear hanging from our 81st-floor balcony. I—I lost it, sir, and I began pounding away on his fingers, but he wouldn't let go so I grabbed my hammer and boy he let go then! He fell, but God must have loved him because somehow he *survived*! So, I grabbed the refrigerator, carried it to the balcony, and threw it down onto him! Yeah, let's see him survive that, right? Unfortunately, the stress of it all was too much for my body and I had a heart attack and died."

"I'm so sorry." Saint Peter exclaimed before turning to the next man. "What happened to you?"

"Well, sir, I was in my apartment on the 82nd floor of my building, riding my stationary exercise bike in nothing but my underwear—I don't like doing more laundry than I absolutely have to. Now, when I exercise I put the bike out on my balcony so I can enjoy the fresh air, plus it's cooler on my body. Well, I was really going at it. I mean, I pushed myself to the absolute limit. When I got done I stood up off of my bike but my legs were really weak and I couldn't catch my balance. Before I know it, I've tripped and gone over the side of my balcony.

"I got lucky, though, because I was able to catch myself on the balcony of the apartment below me. Before I could shout for help, though, some *madman* comes storming out and beating on my fingers. But hey, I manage to hold on and I begin to think I just might make it after all. But then this fucking *lunatic* grabs a claw-hammer and just murders my fingers. I fall, but God must have loved me because I survived. However, as I stand up I look up and *Bam!* This giant refrigerator comes crashing down on top of me and kills me instantly!"

"Wow, buddy, that's rough." Saint Peter comments, turning to the last guy, who is wearing the same suit he was born in. "What about you?"

"Imagine this, Saint Peter, dude. I'm *butt* naked and hiding inside of this woman's refrigerator..."

The Divorced Virgin

A lawyer recently married a woman who had been divorced ten different times. On their wedding night, however, she told her new groom to be gentle, revealing to him that she was still a virgin.

"How is that even possible?" He asked, obviously confused. "You've been married *ten* different times."

"Well," She explained. "Beau was a sales representative; he kept telling me how good it was going to be but in the end he just couldn't deliver. Adam was in software services; he was never really sure how it functioned but he said he'd look into it and get back to me. Kevin was from field services. He claimed everything checked out diagnostically but he just couldn't get the system up.

"Ethan was in telemarketing. Even though he knew he had the order he didn't know when he'd be able to deliver. Tim was an engineer: he understood the basic process but he wanted three years to research, design, and implement a new state-of-the-art method. Terry was from finance and administration: he thought he knew how but he wasn't sure whether or not it was his job.

"David was in marketing—although he had a nice product he was never quite sure how to position it. Darrell was a psychologist: all he ever did was talk about it. Corey was a gynecologist: all he ever did was talk about it. Trey was a stamp collector; all he ever did was—*God,* I miss him!

"But now, I've married you."

"What does that mean?"

"Well, you're a lawyer."

"So?"

"Well, this time I *know* I'm gonna get screwed!"

The Drunken Taxi Ride

To celebrate Paul's upcoming marriage—and to lament his pending demise as a bachelor—Mark and John decided to take their friend out for a night on the town for his bachelor party. By the time the three were ready to head home, however, they were each incredibly and utterly drunk. Barely able to stand up straight, one of the men did the smart thing and hailed a taxi.

As the three men enter the taxi the driver notices immediately that they're all drunk. Smiling, he waits until they're in and then he starts the engine. The driver then waits three seconds and turns his car off.

"We're here, gentlemen." He announces. Paul hands him a $100 bill and gets out. Mark hands the driver a $50 bill, thanks him, and gets out. As he's getting out, though, John stops and then reaches forward, slapping the driver in the back of the head.

"Ouch! I-I-what was *that* for?!" The driver stammers, afraid that John might have realized his trick.

"Watch your speed next time, you damn fool!" John barks in anger. "You almost killed us!"

The Gambler

Eric walked into his local tavern late one evening and took his usual seat at the end of the bar. As usual, he ordered his first beer of the night and then followed it up with his favorite liquor: Scotch.

After about an hour the old war veteran was well and drunk. Laughing loudly at a buddy's joke, he called the bartender over to him.

"Adam, you a bettin' man?"

"I've been known to lay money down from time-to-time: what you got?"

"I bet you $10 I can bite my eye."

Adam thought about it for a minute and then nodded. "What the hell?" After all, this was something that might be worth seeing, and if it didn't work he would be $10 richer.

The two men shook hands to legitimize the wager and then Eric, without missing a beat, took out his glass eye, placed it between his teeth, and bit down. Laughing at the act, Adam handed over the cash as promised.

"Tell you what, Adam; I'll give you a chance to win your money back." Eric announced, placing the money on the bar next to his drink.

"What do you mean?"

"I bet you $20 I can bite my other eye."

Adam considered his odds. It was clear that Eric wasn't blind so obviously his trick wouldn't work twice. Feeling confident, Adam accepted the wager. Eric, in turn, took out his dentures and used his hands to make them bite down on his good eye. Clearly out-maneuvered, Adam shook his head but handed over the money.

"Got one more for you, Adam."

"What?"

"I bet you $100 I can stand on top of this end of the bar, piss over your head, and hit one of those shot glasses behind you without getting a single drop on you."

Initially Adam was cautious: after all, he'd already lost $30 despite having been confident both times. While thinking, however, Eric climbed up onto the end of the bar, nearly falling off and then toppling over in his drunken state.

Adam accepted the wager: there'd be no way on Earth that Eric would succeed this time. With their third handshake of the night Eric dropped his pants, pulled out his penis, aimed, and began to urinate all over the place. By the time the drunk was finished Adam, the bar, several of their customers, and hundreds of dollars of liquor were drenched in piss.

Adam began to laugh, jumping up and down with glee as he cheered his victory. As Adam was screaming, laughing, and smiling, Eric pulled up his pants and climbed down from the bar.

"Why are you smiling so big for, Adam?"

Ha! You owe me $100! I—" Adam froze, seeing a smile on Eric's face that was even bigger than his own. "You just lost $100; why are *you* smiling?"

"I lost $100 to you, sure, but I bet that big city lawyer over by the door $10,000 that I could get drunk, piss all over you, and you'd be *happy* about it!"

The Ugly Baby

A woman had just boarded a bus while carrying her newborn baby in her arms. As she passed the driver, however, he caught her attention.

"Ma'am, meaning no offense but *damn*! That is the *ugliest* baby I've ever seen!"

Appalled, the woman turns around and gets off the bus, almost in tears as she disembarks.

"Ma'am?" A bystander asks, quickly approaching her. "What's wrong?"

"The driver of this bus just insulted me!"

"Well, ma'am, don't run off."

"Huh?"

"Yeah, you just get right back on that bus and tell him off. Go on, now, and don't worry." He added, reaching for her baby. "I'll hold your pet monkey for you."

Two Assholes

My name's Jason and I love to have fun. Now, I don't mean going out and partying every night—that's too stereotypical and only something desperate women or young boys think about. No, my fun is often much more expansive, significantly more inclusive, and—more often than not—much more interruptive.

Perhaps my greatest moment, however, came back in the early '90s, shortly after I'd landed my first major promotion. I'd been sitting at my desk at work (I'd just become a regional bank manager) when I suddenly remembered a phone call I'd forgotten to make. I dug through my desk, found the number, and decided to go ahead and rectify this mistake. After a couple of rings a man answered the other end with a gruff voice. "Hello?"

"Yes, this is Jason with Second National Bank. Could I speak with Joanne Carter, please?"

I am then greeted with a manic voice screaming through the speaker with such force that I nearly went deaf. "GET THE

RIGHT FUCKING NUMBER!" And before I could muster a response I hear that telltale sound of a phone being slammed down.

So rude!

My first order of business afterwards was to track down Joanne's correct number. Upon finding it, I realized that I'd reversed the last four digits of her telephone number. I called her and effortlessly concluded my business with her; one of the easiest phone calls of my life. After we'd hung up, I decided that I should have a spot of fun before the day was up. Thus, I decided to call the "wrong" number again. When the same rude man answered the phone, I screamed out "YOU'RE AN ASSHOLE!" and then I hung up.

I then wrote his number of a separate pad of paper with the word "Asshole" next to it and kept it in my top desk drawer. Every week or so, when I'd have to pay a bill, got bored, or had a bad day and needed my spirits to be lifted up, I'd call him up and scream out "YOU'RE AN ASSHOLE!" and then I'd quickly hang up.

This never failed to cheer me up.

Several months later Caller ID was introduced with explosive popularity. I just knew that my therapy sessions with the Asshole would have to stop. So, late one afternoon I called him.

"'Hello?"

"Yes, this is Ray Vance with the phone company. I'm calling to see if you're familiar with our new Caller ID technology that allows you to see who's calling you *before* you answer your phone."

"No, now goodbye!" And once again the phone was slammed down. I smiled. The fun didn't have to stop.

A few weeks later my wife asked me to stop by the grocery store on my way home from the bank. I'd had to circle the parking lot four different times before at last finding a place to park. However, an old farmer's pickup truck was getting ready to pull out, so I had to sit and wait. As soon as the spot was free I moved forward—and before I'd even recognized what was happening a black BMW cut me off and practically flew into the empty spot. I hit my horn and yelled at him that *I'd* been waiting for that parking spot, but he ignored me and went on into the store.

At this point I noticed a "For Sale" sign in the back window, and so I grabbed a pen and a slip of paper and I wrote down his telephone number. Now I had another asshole to call when I got bored or got down.

A few days later, shortly after calling the original asshole (at this point I had his number on speed dial) I figured I better call the BMW asshole as well.

"Hello?"

"Yes," I asked. "Is this the man with the black BMW for sale?"

"Yes, it is."

"Could you tell me where I can come see it?"

"Yes, sir. I live at 34 Oak Boulevard, in Fairfax. It's a yellow ranch house and the car's parked right out front."

"And what was your name, again?"

"Don." He answered. "Don Jackson."

"When's a good time to catch you, Don?"

"I'm home every evening after 5:00."

"Excellent. Listen, Don, can I tell you something?"

"What's that?"

"Don, you're an asshole!" I exclaimed before hanging up. I then added his number to speed dial too. Now, whenever I had a problem or a bad day I had *two* assholes to call.

And then one day, not long after this, I came up with what will always be the greatest idea I've ever had. I called my first asshole.

"Hello?"

"You're an asshole!" I shouted, only this time I didn't hang up.

"Are you still there?" He asked uncertainly.

"Yeah."

"Stop calling me!"

"Make me!" I retorted, trying my very best not to laugh at this point.

"Who are you?!"

"I'm Don Jackson of 34 Oak Boulevard in Fairfax. I live in a yellow ranch house with a black Beamer out front."

"I'm on my way over now, Don, so you better say your prayers!"

"Yeah, like I'm scared of some little girl, you stupid asshole!" And I hung up.

Smiling like a kid on Christmas morning I then called up ol' Don.

"Hello?" He asked.

"Hello, asshole."

"I swear to God if I ever find out who you are I'll—"

"You'll *what?*"

"I'll kick your ass!"

"Well, asshole, here's your chance; I'm on my way over now!"

And then I hung up. Immediately after talking to Don I called the police, saying that I lived at 34 Oak Boulevard in Fairfax and that I was on my way home to kill my gay lover.

I then called both of our local news stations and told them about the gang war going down at 34 Oak Boulevard in Fairfax.

Once that final call was made I quickly got in my car and drove home, where I grabbed my wife (almost literally) and got her into the car as well. We then drove over to Fairfax.

We arrived just in time to watch two assholes beating the crap out of each other while surrounded by police cars and SWAT vans, all while a news helicopter circled overhead and four different news crews surrounded the scene.

Man, life was so much better in the '90s.

Worse Things

Late one afternoon Steve got the rare chance to leave work early and so he decided to just go on home and call it a day a little earlier than normal. When he got home he went upstairs to his room to get some fresh clothes, but as he passed his daughter's room he stopped, something rather unusual having just caught his attention through the crack of the bedroom door.

Pushing the door open Steve was astounded to see that Stacy had made her bed—after inspecting the bed Steve was even willing to admit it could pass a drill sergeant's judgment. As a father he found himself quite proud of his little girl. That pride, however, soon turned into fear and trepidation as he noticed an envelope propped up prominently against the pillow. A sense of foreboding gripping his heart, Steve picked the letter up, turned it over in his hands, and then decided to open it, his hands trembling.

Dear Mom and Dad,

It's with great regret and sorrow that I'm writing you. I have eloped with my new boyfriend, but I couldn't tell you in person because I wanted to avoid causing too much of a scene.

I've been finding real passion with George. He's kind, caring, and nice, but I knew nonetheless that you'd never approve of him. I knew you'd never accept all of his tattoos, piercings, the tight motorcycle clothes he always wears, and because he's so much older than I am: while 45 is just another number to me I know you'd not agree.

But Dad, Mom, it's not only passion—I'm pregnant. George has promised me that the three of us will be very happy together. He owns a trailer deep in the woods and he already has a stack of firewood to get us through the coming winter. We also share a dream of having many more children together.

George has really opened my eyes to the fact that marijuana really doesn't hurt anyone; it's only illegal because it can't be adequately taxed. We'll be growing it ourselves, now, and trading it with the other members of our commune for all of the food, cocaine, and pain killers we need for ourselves and our growing family.

In the meantime we'll continue to pray that science finds a cure for AIDS so that George gets better; he sure deserves it!

Dad, Mom, please don't worry about me: I'm 14 and I know how to take care of myself. I'm sure someday we'll come back home so that you can visit your many, many grandchildren.

Your Loving Daughter,

Stacy

P.S. Mom, Dad, none of the above is true—I'm over at Alice's house. I just wanted to remind you that there are much worse things in life besides the report card waiting for you on the kitchen table. Please call Alice's house when it's safe for me to come back home.

Wrong Email

Robert and Julie were a happily-married couple from Minnesota. During one unusually-arctic winter they decided to take some time off from life and take a vacation to Florida so that they could thaw out and celebrate their coming wedding anniversary. To add some much-wanted romance they even decided to stay at the same hotel where they'd spent their honeymoon three decades ago. However, because of their hectic schedules it was nearly impossible to coordinate their travel plans. Eventually, it was decided that Robert would fly down to the Sunshine State on Thursday while Julie would join him the next day.

Upon arrival Robert checked into the hotel. When he reached their room, however, he noticed that a lot had changed since thirty years ago. Chief among these changes was the computer now in the room. After getting himself situated he decided to send an email to his beloved wife to let her know that he'd made it safely. Unfortunately, in his excitement he misspelled her email address and did not notice this mistake before sending the email through.

Meanwhile, over in Houston, an old woman had just returned home. Her husband, a Baptist minister, had just been laid to rest following his death from a massive heart attack days earlier. That evening she was getting ready for bed when she decided to check her email. Her husband had been a well-respected and well-liked man so she knew her inbox would be full with consolations from friends and well-wishers. Upon opening the first email, however, she screamed and passed out. Her son rushed into the bedroom where he noticed his mother sprawled out upon the carpet. He then looked up, noticing the email open on her computer screen.

The email read:

To: My Most Loving Wife
Subject: I've Arrived
Date: July 13, 2012

Hello, dear. I bet you're surprised to hear from me, aren't you? It's really amazing—they have computers here now and you're allowed to send emails to your loved ones! I just wanted to let you know I've arrived and have been checked in.

Everything's been prepared for your arrival tomorrow. I'm really looking forward to seeing you again. I hope your trip is as quick and uneventful as mine was.

P.S. It sure is friggin' hot down here.

Short Jokes

A Woman & a Yeast Infection

Question: What do you call an anorexic woman with a yeast infection?

Answer: A Quarter-Pounder with Cheese

Breaking Up With Ruth

I just texted my girlfriend, Ruth, and told her that it's over between us. I told her exactly how I was feeling. It made her cry but I don't care.

I guess you can say I'm Ruthless.

Cemetery Walls

Question: Why do so many cemeteries keep a fence or wall around them?

Answer: Because people are dying to get in.

Cow Magazines

Question: What kind of magazines do cows read?

Answer: Cattlelogs

In the Wrong Body

When I was extremely young I always felt like I was a man trapped in a woman's body.

But then I was born.

Kangaroo & The Empire State Building

Question: Can a Kangaroo jump higher than the Empire State Building?

Answer: Of course it can: the Empire State Building can't jump.

My Ex & The Titanic

Question: What's the difference between my ex-girlfriend and the *Titanic?*

Answer: The Titanic only went down on 1,000 people.

Rihanna & Chris Brown

Question: How did Rihanna find out that Chris Brown was cheating on her?

Answer: She found another woman's lipstick on his knuckles.

Sex & Bridge

Question: How is sex like a game of Bridge?

Answer: If you have a great hand you don't need a partner.

Sperm & Egg

Question: Why does it take one million of a man's sperm cells to fertilize one egg?

Answer: Because they won't stop to ask for directions.

Surprise Party

After several years it dawned on me one day that my parents favored my twin brother over me. How, do you ask? They asked me to help blow up balloons for his surprise birthday party.

The Depressed Wife

It's been raining for more than three days now, and to be honest my wife is starting to grow rather depressed. I've tried ignoring it but it's become too much. I mean, she's just standing there, looking through the window. I tell you, if it doesn't stop raining tomorrow I'll have to let her in.

The Dwarf

On my way to work this morning I got distracted listening to the radio and so ended up rear-ending another car as it sat at a red light. The driver got out and it was at that point that I saw he was a dwarf.

"I'm not Happy." He said with a frown.

"Well then," I asked. "Which one are you?"

The Greeter

Two hours into my first day on the job as a Wal-Mart greeter, the ugliest woman I'd ever seen came in with her two kids in tow and holding her hands. As I listened I could hear the woman cussing and snapping at them like they were nothing more than stray dogs trespassing in her yard. As it continued it quickly reached the point that I could no longer just stand by. I walked up to her.

"Good morning! Welcome to Wal-Mart!" I greeted quite happily. "Those are beautiful kids—are they twins?"

The woman glared daggers at me. "Hell, no, they ain't twins!" She snapped. "One's 9 and the other's 5! Why in the hell would you think they're twins?! Are you blind, or stupid?!"

I chuckled. "No, ma'am, I'm neither blind nor stupid. It's just—well, I just couldn't believe someone willingly had sex with you twice. Have a good day, now, and again thanks for shopping at Wal-Mart."

My supervisor later told me I probably wasn't cut out for this line of work.

Titanic Warning

My grandfather tried to warn them about the *Titanic;* he knew immediately that there was trouble. He kept screaming and shouting at them that the ship was going to sink well before it did. However, all they did was throw him out of the theater.

University of Tennessee

QUESTION: Why is the University of Tennessee's school color orange?

ANSWER: So that the locals can go hunting on Saturday, go to the game on Sunday, and pick up trash along the roads on Monday.

Walking Down the Street

I was walking down the street the other day and I punched a white guy. The police came along and arrested me for Assault. That next day I was again walking down the street, but this time I punched a black man. Again, the police arrived shortly afterwards, but this time they arrested me for Impersonating a Police Officer.

50 Bad & Funny Puns

1. The man who invented the door-knocker won the Nobel Peace Prize.

2. When I get naked in the bathtub the shower always gets turned on.

3. Having sex in an elevator is wrong on so many levels.

4. People who claim it sucks to be constipated are full of shit.

5. If Apple made a car, would it have Windows?

6. I was wondering why the ball was getting bigger. Then it hit me.

7. Light travels faster than the speed of sound. That's why some people appear bright until you hear them speak.

8. I have a few jokes about unemployed people, but none of them ever work.

9. "I have multiple personalities." Said Tom, being Frank.

10.   Will glass coffins be a success? Remains to be seen.

11.   How do you make Holy Water? You boil the hell out of it.

12. What's the difference between a Hippo and a Zippo? One is really heavy and the other is a little lighter.

13. I lost my job at the bank on my very first day. A woman asked me to check her balance, so I pushed her over.

14. Two windmills are standing on a wind farm. One asks "What's your favorite kind of music?" The other answers "I'm a big metal fan."

15. The man who survived pepper spray and mustard gas is now a seasoned veteran.

16. I tried suing the airline for losing my luggage. I lost my case.

17. Jill broke her finger today, but on the other hand she was completely fine.

18. A cross-eyed teacher just couldn't control his pupils.

19. Is it ignorance or apathy that's destroying the world today? I don't know and really don't care.

20. Allow me to tell you about my grandfather. He was a good man, and a brave man. He had the heart of a lion—and a life-long ban from the zoo.

21. Which nation has the fastest-growing population of its capital? Ireland: every day it's Dublin.

22.   Originally I wasn't going to get a brain transplant, but I changed my mind.

23.   What do you get when mix liquor and literature? Tequila Mockingbird.

24.   How do you throw a space-themed party? You planet.

25.   There was a kidnapping at the school yesterday. Luckily he woke up.

26.   My ex-wife still misses me, but her aim is improving.

27.   Saturday and Sunday are the strongest days of the week; the rest are weekdays.

28.   What's the difference between a properly-dressed man on a bicycle and a nicely-dressed man on a tricycle? A tire.

29.   I saw an ad for burial plots, but that's the last thing I need.

30.   German sausage jokes are the wurst.

31.   I always try to make chemistry jokes but I never get a reaction.

32.   Sleeping comes so naturally to me that I can do it with my eyes closed.

33.   Need an ark? I Noah guy.

34.   How does Moses make coffee? Hebrews it.

35.   I walked into my sister's room and tripped on a bra; it was a booby trap.

36.   I just burned 2,000 calories: that's the last time I nap while I have brownies in the oven.

37.   Most people are shocked when they find out how bad I am as an electrician.

38.   My girlfriend left me so I took her wheelchair. Guess who came crawling back.

39.   Don't trust atoms; they make up everything.

40.   I bought some shoes from a drug dealer. I don't know what he laced them with but I've been tripping all day.

41.   I couldn't quite remember how to throw a boomerang, but eventually it came back to me.

42.   A courtroom artist was arrested today, but details are sketchy.

43.   I worked in the woods as a lumberjack but I couldn't hack it, so they gave me the axe.

44.   My first job was at an orange juice factory but I soon got canned: I couldn't concentrate.

45.   My wife told me she wanted to end our marriage because she's tired of all the *Star Wars* puns. I responded "Divorce is strong with this one."

46. For Halloween we dressed up as almonds. People could tell we were nuts.

47. A man who runs behind a car will get exhausted, but a man who runs in front of a car will get tired.

48. What do you call a cow with no legs? Ground Beef.

49. I feel sorry for the depressed plumber; he's been going through some shit.

50. I know smoking is bad for you, but I was raised to never be a quitter.

A Girl From Mississippi

Question: What do you call a girl from Mississippi who can outrun her brothers and cousins?

Answer: A Virgin

A Redneck & an Elevator

Question: What's the difference between a Redneck and an Elevator?

Answer: An elevator can successfully raise a child.

Alabama's State Motto

Did you hear about Alabama's new state motto?

Alabama: the state with fifteen million people and fifteen last names.

Redneck Murder Scene

Question: What do cops hate the most about a Redneck murder scene?

Answer: All of the DNA samples match and there are no dental records.

Redneck Wives

Every single time I look at my wife I can't help but remember just how lucky I am. It's good enough when she loves you for who you are and tolerates all of your flaws, but when she also looks like your favorite country music singer—well, that's truly something special.

To make it even better, my best friend's wife looks just like *his* favorite country singer and she's just as loving and tolerant of him as my missus is of me.

At least—this is what I thought before that accident at the mall last week. I went to use the public bathroom and when I came out they'd done gone and gotten into a catfight. As if that's not bad enough I heard some old man scream "HOLY SHIT! WILLIE NELSON'S KICKING TOBY KEITH'S ASS!"

Blonde Jokes

Florida & the Moon

Two blondes, Christie and Jane, were standing out in Christie's backyard at her Oklahoma City home, enjoying the crisp autumn weather. Eventually, Jane looks up at the night sky and poses a question she's long had in her mind.

"Which do you think is closer, Florida or the moon?"

"*Duh!*" Christie answers immediately. "Can you see Florida from here?"

The Blonde & the TV

Samantha had always dreamt of the day she'd be rich and could buy anything she wanted. One day, her uncle died and, as she was his favorite niece, he left his entire estate—all of his fortune and life's work—to her. At last, she could make her dreams come true.

A few days later she walked into a local store and began browsing for things she could add to her new home. After an hour of walking around and browsing, she found that one item that she just could *not* live without. All smiles and bouncing with excitement, she walked up to the register. There, she pointed at the object that had become her heart's desire.

"Sir, I'd like to buy that television set over there."

"Ma'am, I'm sorry but we don't sell to blondes. Please leave now."

Heartbroken, Samantha left, but she refused to be deterred so easily. The next day she returned, this time sporting a red wig. She paused before exiting her taxi, checking herself in the side mirror. Her smile grew—there was no way that cashier would recognize her.

She entered the store and walked herself to the register, again pointing at her heart's desire. "Sir, I'd like to purchase that television set sitting there."

The cashier rolled his eyes. "Ma'am, I told you yesterday; we don't sell to blondes. Now, please leave."

She wheeled and huffed off, yet she still refused to give up. And so the next day she returned yet again, now sporting a brown wig. Satisfied that this time she'd get him, she walked up to the front counter.

"Pardon me, young man, but I surely would like to buy that there T.V."

Again, he rolled his eyes. "Ma'am, this is the third time I've said this; we *don't* sell to blondes. Now leave."

Angry, she jerked the wig off of her head, threw it to the floor, and stormed out. Yet, she still refused to give in. That night, thus, she concocted the perfect plan. She shaved her head, glued a fake beard and mustache to her face, and with the help of two friends, a corset, and shoulder pads beneath a suit and tie, she was at last ready.

The next morning, she returned for her next try. She stepped through the door and swaggered her way to the register, walking as though she owned the store.

"I'm here for that television set." She explained. "How much?"

The cashier at last snapped. "Listen here, stupid! I've told you three times and I'm *not* going to tell you again. No matter how hard you try, we *don't* sell to blondes. Now leave, and if you come back I'm calling the cops!"

"How'd you know it was me?!" She bellowed, unable to believe her luck.

"Ma'am?"

"What?!"

"That's not a television—that's a microwave."

The Blonde in the Desert

A plane crashed while crossing a desert, and only three people—all women—survived. One woman was a redhead, the second was a brunette, and the third was a blonde.

For several hours the women wandered aimlessly across the sandy, dusty landscape, looking for any sign of relief or salvation. Finally, after what seemed like years, the ladies came across an ancient-looking lamp. The women passed it amongst themselves, wondering what they should do now. Jokingly, the blonde suggested they all rub the lamp to see if a magic genie would come out and grant them each three wishes. Deciding that failure would do nothing to worsen their situation, the women agreed and so the each placed a hand on the lamp and rubbed.

Sure enough, a genie erupted from the spout in a puff of dark, purple smoke. Surveying his new masters, he nodded his head.

"I am indebted to you for my release, my masters, and thus I am sworn to provide three wishes to whomever shall free me. As there are three of you, however, you may each have one wish and no more. You cannot wish for immortality or for more wishes."

"I wish I was back at home with my family." The redhead declared immediately. The genie bowed his head and snapped his fingers and in a puff of green smoke the redhead was gone.

"I wish I was back in my Jacuzzi with a nice margarita." The brunette lamented. Again, the genie bowed his head and snapped his fingers. In a puff of green smoke, the brunette disappeared.

"Awww shucks, now I'm lonely." The blonde cried. "I wish those two were back here with me!"

Three Blondes on an Island

One fateful day three blondes found themselves trapped on a deserted island with no technology in sight. With no way to contact the outside world nor any way to escape their predicament, the ladies agreed that their wisest move would be to explore the island and see if they could find anything that might aide them in their quest to return home.

After several hours, the trio came across a half-buried lamp. Laughing, they nonetheless agree to rub the lamp to see if a genie might pop out—after all, it worked in the movies. To their elated surprise, their plan worked. In a puff of purple-blue smoke, the genie rose high above them, looking down upon his newest masters with a friendly enough smile.

"I usually grant upon the finder of my lamp three wishes!" His deep voice boomed outwards. "However, as there are three of you I shall instead grant you each single wish. You cannot wish for immortality or for more wishes, so choose your wish wisely."

After much thought, the first blond steps forward.

"Mr. Genie, sir, I wish I was smart enough to figure a way off of this island."

The genie nods. "As you wish it so shall it be!"

In a puff of white smoke he turns her into a redhead and she then proceeds to swim off the island.

The second blond steps forward. "I wish I was even smarter so I could find a way off this island."

The genie nods again. "As you wish."

In a puff of white smoke he turns her into a brunette and she then proceeds to build a raft and sail off.

The third blonde never hesitates. "I wish I was smarter than both of them *combined* so I could find a way off this island!"

"As my master wishes so shall it be." The genie booms. In a puff of white smoke the third blonde is turned into a man and he walks across the bridge.

Two Blondes in a Hole

Two blondes were walking through a park late one afternoon when they both fell into a deep hole. Once they reached the bottom the first blonde looked up at the tiny pin-prick of light.

"It sure is dark in here, isn't it?"

"I don't know." The other blonde responded. "I can't see."

Political Jokes

Sleeping With Bill

When asked if they would have sex with Bill Clinton, 95% of women in D.C. answered with "Not again."

A Criminal President

Back in 2016 Donald Trump said that if I voted for Hillary Clinton I'd be stuck with a criminal President under constant federal investigation from Day One.

Turns out, he was right.

I voted for Hillary Clinton and I've been stuck with a criminal President under constant federal investigation since Day One.

A Tragedy

A Little Johnny Story

One morning Donald Trump made a surprise visit to a local Washington, D.C. elementary school. Part of his visit involved him sitting in on one of the classes. While in this class, Mr. Trump got involved in a discussion on various words and their meanings as a part of their lessons. Ms. Cook then asked Trump if he'd like to lead the discussion on the word "tragedy". Donald agreed to do so and he begun by asking the class for an example of the word "tragedy" in a sentence.

Little Ed stood up and says "If my best friend is playing in the field of his family's farm and a runaway tractor comes along and runs over and kills him that would be a tragedy."

"No." Mr. Trump corrected. "That would be an accident."

Little Sarah then stood up. "If a school bus carrying forty children drove off a cliff, killing everyone inside, that would be a tragedy."

"I'm afraid not." Donald explained. "That's what we would call a great lost."

The room fell silent as the students contemplated this lesson. As the silence deepens, Trump looked around the room and said, a little testily, "Isn't there *anyone* here who can give me an example of a tragedy?"

At last, a little boy in the back stood up. Immediately, Ms. Cook stepped forward even as Donald pointed to the boy.

"Yes?"

"W—"

"That's enough, Johnny: go ahead and sit down. I'm sorry, Mr. President, but Johnny tends to give answers that aren't always the *nicest*—"

"That's alright; I want to hear what he says. Go ahead, little Johnny: what's your answer?"

"If Air Force One was struck by a missile and blown to smithereens while you're onboard, Mr. Trump, that would be a real tragedy."

"Fantastic!" Donald Trump explained. "That's exactly right! Now, can you tell me why that would be a tragedy?"

"Well," Johnny answered. "It would *have* to be a tragedy, because it definitely wouldn't be a great loss and it sure as hell wouldn't be an accident, either."

Going Red

Did you hear about Monica Lewinsky becoming a Republican? That last Democrat left a bad taste in her mouth.

If She Wasn't His Daughter

To be honest, I really can't see why people were so outraged when Donald Trump said that if Ivanka wasn't his daughter he'd date her.

After all, if Ivanka wasn't Trump's daughter I'd date her too.

Lie Clocks

Alan died one day and before long he found himself standing at the Pearly Gates. As he was speaking with St. Peter he noticed a titanic wall behind him, lined with clocks for as far as the eye could see. Alan couldn't resist his curiosity.

"What are all of those clocks?"

"Those are Lie Clocks." St. Peter explained. "Every human to ever live has a Lie Clock; every time you lie the hand on the clock will move."

"Oh, okay." He exclaimed before pointing to a clock with both hands still at 12 o'clock. "Whose clock is that?"

"That was Mother Teresa's. The hands have never moved, meaning that she never told a lie." St. Peter explained before pointing to another clock. "And that belonged to Abraham Lincoln. His hand only moved twice, indicating he only ever told two lies. And then there's Barack Obama's clock; as you can see he only ever told eight lies."

"St. Peter?"

"Yes?"

"Where's President Trump's clock?"

"Oh, *his* is God's office."

"Because God's so proud of his honesty and integrity?"

St. Peter laughed. "Nah—God's just using it as a ceiling fan."

Presidential Heaven

George W. Bush, Barack Obama, and Donald Trump die and go to Heaven. When they reach the Pearly Gates, however, they're met by St. Peter, who's standing there with a frown on his face.

"I'm sorry, gentlemen." He explains. "But Heaven's starting to get quite crowded, so we can't let just anyone in."

"Then what do we do?" Asks President Obama.

"Well, I'm going to take you to talk to God, and He'll decide who gets in and who goes to Hell."

The three men agree that this is acceptable and so they follow St. Peter into Heaven, through the streets of gold, and then up to the Celestial Throne where God was sitting. St. Peter made the introductions and then walked off, leaving God to deal with His three new arrivals.

"I want to hear in your own words why you think I should let you in, why you deserve to be in Heaven. So, George, you first."

"Well, Lord, I've not always been the greatest man but I've always tried to do what I think is right, even if I sometimes end up in the wrong. On September 11 I kept my nation and my people together through the darkest hour of our nation's history, and I've gone out of my way to take care of the men and women I sent into harm's way."

God nods, agreeing that He can't really argue that point. He then turns to the next man. "Barack, what about you? Why do you think I should let you into Heaven?"

"Well, God, I agree that George always did what he thought was best, though he did take some less-than-stellar advice and made decisions that financially ruined America. But, you know, I never gave up on the American Dream and I did everything I possibly could to put her back on the right track when I took office, even when half of my government refused to do their job. It was hard, but I feel like America's better off because of my time in office."

Again, God nodded. "I agree—your leadership also helped save the Union." And then God turned to Donald Trump, ignoring the smug look on the man's face. "And what about you, Donald? What do *you* think?"

"Well—uh—I-I think—I think you're sitting in my chair."

Trump Changes the Light Bulb

Question: How long does it take Donald Trump to change the light bulb?

Look, we can change the light bulb, okay? That I *will* tell you. We're changing it, okay? And I understand what you're saying, I hear it all the time. People—they call me and say "Is the light bulb really dead?" That's what they are asking me. It's unbelievable. The light bulb is in big trouble, that I can tell you. But we are going to change it.

U.N. Survey

A worldwide survey was recently conducted by the United Nations. The only question asked was **"Would you please give your honest opinion about solutions to the food shortage in the rest of the world?"**

Suffice it to say, this survey was a massive failure. Why?

In Africa, they didn't know what **"food"** meant. In Eastern Europe they didn't know what **"honest"** meant. In Western Europe they didn't know what **"shortage"** meant. The Chinese didn't know what **"opinion"** meant, and in the Middle East they didn't know what **"solution"** meant. In South America they didn't know what **"please"** meant, and in the United States they didn't know what **"the rest of the world"** meant.

Yellow Snow

Bright one winter morning Donald Trump stepped out onto the front lawn of the White House, admiring the beautiful snow that had fallen the night before. Almost immediately, however, his smile turned upside down as he noticed the sight that greeted him.

There on the ground, were the words "Donald Trump Sucks" written in urine on top of the snow.

Immediately, he found himself growing angry. Storming back into the White House he walked to the security center responsible for ensuring the White House is safe. He walked in and began yelling at his security chief.

"Somebody wrote an insult directed at me on the front lawn! And to make it even worse, they wrote it in *piss*! Whoever did it had to be standing right there when he did it! Where were you guys?!"

The security chief says nothing but instead stares at the floor, ashamed. Trump screamed again.

"Well dammit, don't just stand there! Get out there and find out who did it! And I want answers *tonight*!"

The entire security staff immediately explodes into action, people running for the exits as they make to comply with Trump's demands.

Later that evening, his security chief finds Donald just after finishing dinner. The chief approaches slowly and says "Well, Mr. President, we have some bad news and then we have some *really* bad news. Which do you want first?"

Trump sighs. "Give me the bad news first."

"Well, we took a sample of the urine and tested it. The results just returned, and it—it was Mike Pence's urine."

Trump's face fall. "Oh my God, I-I f-feel so—so—so betrayed! My own Vice-President! Damn! Well, what's the really bad news?"

"Well, Mr. President—it was Melania's handwriting."

Cop & Military Jokes

Speeding

Lacey was late getting off of work one night and in a hurry to get home to her loving husband and children she put more pressure on the gas pedal than she'd realized. As she failed to stifle a yawn blue lights began to flash behind her, and only too late did she realize her mistake. Chastising herself for her foolishness, she pulled over and waited for the officer to approach her window. Sure enough, moments later she was face-to-face with a young, fresh-faced police officer. It was all she could do not to smile.

"Evening, ma'am."

"Is there a problem, Officer?"

He nodded. "The reason I pulled you over, ma'am, is that you were doing 55 in a 35. Is everything okay?"

"I—I think it is, yeah."

"Okay. Can I see your license?"

"Well, if I had one I'd definitely give it to you."

"You don't have a driver's license?"

"No sir—I lost it for the fourth time for driving while intoxicated."

"I see. Well, go ahead and get me your registration and we'll go from there."

"Well you see, Officer, I can't really do that."

"Why not?"

"I stole this car."

"You stole—you *stole* it?"

"Yes, sir, right after I killed the owner."

"You *killed* the owner?"

"Sure did; got him with this revolver under my seat. He's in the trunk if you want to see."

At this point the Officer instructs Lacey to sit in the car before slowly, *cautiously* returning to his patrol car. Not even five minutes later a helicopter's hovering right above her as a dozen police vehicles surround her from all sides.

Still not smiling, Lacey watches as a man who can only be someone high up the chain-of-command approaches her car, his hand on his pistol.

"Ma'am, could you please place your left hand out of your window and open the door with your right hand?"

Lacey cooperates, doing exactly as instructed. Once out, she holds her hands as high over her head as she can manage.

"Ma'am, are you armed?"

"No sir."

"Do you have any weapons in the car?"

"No, sir—I don't even own a gun."

"Do you mind if I check?"

"Go for it." She answered, stepping to the side. The senior officer then checks under the seat but returns empty-handed.

"Is this your car?"

"Sure is."

"Do you have the registration?"

"Yes, sir—it's in the glove compartment."

The senior officer has another cop check and sure enough he returns a minute later with the registration papers.

"Do you have your license on you?"

"Of course—may I get it out of my purse?"

"Sure. And do you mind if I check the trunk?"

"Not at all; be my guest."

While Lacey retrieves her license from her purse the officer checks the trunk. When he returns, she hands him her license. After studying it carefully, he hands it to another officer to run her information.

"Can I ask what's going on, Mr.—"

"Sergeant Nolan." The man introduces himself. "Ma'am, my officer said your license was suspended for DWI, you stole the vehicle, and you killed its owner with a revolver under your seat before hiding his body in the trunk."

"And I bet that motherfucker told you I was speeding, too!"

The Army & the Boy Scouts

Question: What's the difference between the Army and the Boy Scouts?

Answer: The Boy Scouts have adult supervision.

The Definition of Courage

One day the President of the United States decided to hold a meeting with the heads of each branch of the military. It was such a beautiful day that the President decided the meeting should be held outside so as to not let the beauty of the day go to waste. While they were sitting and talking the conversation eventually switched over to the topic of courage and that word's true definition. After some significant discussion, the Commandant of the Coast Guard stood up.

"Gentlemen, I should like to settle this debate right now." And then he proceeded to call one of his men forward. "Petty Officer, I want you to climb the flagpole and then slide back down."

The Petty Officer did as instructed and once he returned to the ground he saluted and walked off.

"That's true courage." The Commandant concluded, sitting back down. The General of the Air Force, however, laughed as he, too, stood up.

"That's nothing." He explained before calling one of his top pilots over. "Lieutenant, I want you to climb the flag pole, sing the national anthem, and then slide back down."

The pilot saluted and then climbed the flag pole. Once at the top, he sang a perfect rendition of the national anthem and then slid back down as instructed. Back on solid ground he then saluted and walked off.

"There's your true courage." The General proclaimed proudly. Shaking his head, the Admiral of the Navy stood up.

"That's nothing." He explained, calling one of his sailors forward. "Seaman, I want you to climb that flag pole blindfolded, sing the national anthem, and then slide back down head-first."

The sailor did as instructed, and once finished he removed the blindfold, saluted, and walked off.

"*There's* your true courage, gentlemen."

"That's horse shit." The General of the Army argued, now taking his turn and calling one of his Privates forward. "Private, you're gonna climb that flag pole blindfolded, in full gear, sing the national anthem, and jump off with a perfect landing."

"Yes, sir!" The private saluted and then proceeded to get into full combat gear. Once blindfolded, he did as instructed and, somehow, managed to jump off and make a perfect landing. He saluted and then walked off.

At this point, however, the Commandant of the Marine Corps was laughing so hard that he was in tears. As the General of the Army took his seat the grizzled old veteran stood up.

"Corporal!" He bellowed. "Front and center!"

A young woman ran up, stopping just in front of her general and offering the crispest salute he'd ever seen.

"Get in full combat gear and fill your bag full of bricks. I want you to then put a blindfold on and stick your combat knife in your mouth. You will then climb the flag pole, sing the national anthem *backwards*, and then jump down head-first."

"Sir!" The young Corporal responded. "Fuck you, sir!"

The old general laughed. "Now *that's* true courage!"

The Traffic Stop

Old Sherman and his beloved wife, Mildred, had been married just over sixty years when Mildred's advanced age at last caught up with her. For the first several weeks Sherman was busy with Mildred's funeral and performing the unenviable task of paying off her final expenses. Eventually, however, things settled down and before too long his life had returned to a daily routine that quickly grew too boring—things just weren't the same without Mildred. One day Sherman had finally had enough with the overwhelming boredom and he decided it was time to do something that he'd always wanted to do as a young man, something he'd never had the chance to do.

Drawing on the significant amount of life insurance money he had left over following Mildred's death, Sherman went to a local car dealership and he brought himself a fancy-looking, fire engine-red convertible sports car. He spared no expense, getting all of the bells and whistles added.

That afternoon, the purchase now complete, Sherman decided to take his new car out onto the interstate to see what the thing was capable of. After several minutes of cruising just above the speed limit he decided, for only the second time in his life, to throw caution into the wind. It was time to forget the rules. He opened up the throttle and put the pedal to the metal. In just seconds his car was topping out at speeds of over one hundred and forty miles per hour. With the top down it was easily the best physical sensation he'd ever felt, the freest he'd ever been.

Soon, however, he saw blue lights flashing in his rearview. He should stop, he knew, but this feeling was just so amazing, so fleeting, that he couldn't bring himself to stop.

No. Forget stopping. It was time, just once, for old Sherman to have some fun. He urged the car forward, the police car behind him only just able to keep him in view.

Only when the nearest city's skyline came into view did Sherman at last decide he'd had his fun. The open road was one thing, but he didn't want to put anyone else at risk by continuing his flight through the city's congested traffic, especially as they were quickly approaching the evening rush hour. Fulfilled, he killed his speed and pulled off onto the shoulder of the highway, turning off his engine as he waited for the cop to come and arrest him.

Moments later, as predicted, a large, bearded, burly state trooper approached his door, his face's heavily-tanned skin wrinkled in an exhausted frown.

"Howdy, Officer."

"Sir, I clocked you at over 150 miles an hour at one point. You refused to yield to an emergency vehicle—I mean, I should already have you in handcuffs—"

"I'm sorry, sir, I—"

"But I've had a *really* long and hard day, my shift's over in ten minutes, and right now I'd much rather be on my way home than going to fill out paperwork, booking a suspect, and filling out even more paperwork because of overtime. So! If you can give me a *damn* good reason for going so fast—something I've *not* heard before—I'll let you off with a warning."

"Well, Officer, you see, years ago I lost my wife—she ran away with a state trooper."

"So? What's that got to do with anything?"

"Well, you see, I was just afraid you were bringing her back to me."

The Officer laughed and then tipped his hat. "Sir, watch that speed and have a safe drive home."

10 Things Not to Say to Cops

1. Sorry, Officer, but I can't reach my license unless you hold my beer.

2. When the cop mentions your eyes look red and asks if you've been drinking, *don't* respond with "Well, your eyes look a little glazed—you been eating donuts?"

3. Sorry Officer—I didn't realize I was driving.

4. Wow! You must've been doing at least 125 miles per hour to keep up with me.

5. I was going to be a cop too but I decided to finish high school instead.

6. You're not gonna check the trunk, are you?

7. It wasn't my fault, Officer, I swear: when I reached down to roll this joint my gun fell out of my lap and got lodged under the brake pedal.

8. I'm sorry, Officer, I was trying to keep up with traffic but it's miles ahead of me.

9. Your mom (or wife) gave me a much better look than that last night.

10.   If I'd known I was getting a full-body cavity search, I'd have waxed first!

Anti-Jokes

A Dog With No Legs

Question: What do you call a dog with no legs?

Answer: It doesn't matter what you call him—he isn't coming.

A Hole in the Heart

Question: What leaves an even bigger hole in your heart than a bad breakup?

Answer: A Bullet

Bad For Your Teeth

Question: What's red and bad for your teeth?

Answer: A brick

Hamsters & Cigarettes

Question: How are hamsters like cigarettes?

Answer: They're completely harmless until you put them in your mouth and light them on fire.

People & Drums

Question: How are people like drums?

Answer: If you hit them with a stick they make a noise.

Axe in the Head

Question: What do you call a man with an axe in his head?

Answer: An ambulance—that's a pretty serious head injury.

Snow Friends

Question: How are friends like snow?

Answer: If you pee on them they disappear.

Tree Friends

Question: What do friends and trees have in common?

Answer: The both fall over if you hit them repeatedly with an axe.

Little Johnny Jokes

A New Vocabulary

A Little Johnny Story

Little Johnny came home from school one day just in time to overhear his parents having a rather heated argument. After they'd both gone their separate ways, Johnny went up to his father.

"Dad, what does **'bitch'** mean?"

"Oh, erm—it's another word to call a lady."

"Oh, okay. What does **'bastard'** mean?"

"Well, son, that's another word for a gentleman."

"Oh, okay, thanks Dad." Little Johnny said, smiling as he went about his way.

The next day, Johnny returned home after school and this time caught his parents having makeup sex. After they'd finished, Johnny went up to his mother.

"Momma, what's a penis?"

"Oh! Well, it—it is another word for a hat."

"Oh, okay. What does **'vagina'** mean?"

"Well, honey, it's another word for a coat."

"Oh, okay, thanks Momma." And so little Johnny went about his way.

The next afternoon Johnny was in the kitchen doing his homework while his grandmother was cooking dinner. However, she cut herself while preparing the chicken and couldn't help but scream. "FUCK!"

"Grandma, what does **'fuck'** mean?"

"Don't worry, Johnny, it's just another word for **'cut'**."

"Thanks, Grandma."

A few weeks later it was Thanksgiving and, to keep him occupied and out of the way while his mother and grandmother prepared the meal, Johnny was assigned to answer the door when the rest of the family from up north arrived.

The doorbell rang and Johnny was quick to open the door, smiling proudly as he greeted his family.

"Hello, and welcome bitches and bastards! Hurry up with your penises and vaginas because Dad can't wait to fuck the turkey!"

Adult Night at School

A Little Johnny Story

One brisk, cloudy afternoon in early November Little Johnny came home from school and went straight out to the garage where his dad was working on his car.

"Hi, daddy, I'm home from school."

"Did you learn anything good today, son?"

"I sure did."

"Well, what'd you learn?"

"That the school's hosting a special adult night tonight."

"An adult night, eh?"

"Yup."

"What's so special about it?"

"It's just gonna you and Miss Cook."

"Just Miss Cook and me, huh? I like the sound of that."

"Yes, sir, just you and Miss Cook. And the principal. And those two police officers."

Heaven or Hell

A Little Johnny Story

One day in class little Johnny was causing quite the commotion. He wouldn't listen, he'd ignore his teacher's commands, and when she'd talk he'd get louder and louder, always ensuring he was talking over her. Finally, poor Ms. Cook was pushed to her limit. She'd had enough.

"That's it, Johnny—after school I'm calling your mother and I'm telling her about your *dreadful* behavior today."

"I'm sorry, Ms. Cook—I'm afraid you can't do that."

"And why not? Hmmm?"

"Well, my mother died years ago."

"Oh, I—"

"But don't worry: when I die and go to Heaven I'll give her the message for you."

And now Ms. Cook smirked. At long-last she finally had the little smartass.

"Yeah, and what if she's in Hell?"

Johnny snorted. "Well hell, then, if that's the case why worry about me? You'll be able to tell her yourself."

Late For Class

A Little Johnny Story

Five minutes after the bell rang for the start of class that morning, the door to Ms. Cook's class opened and little Johnny strode happily to his desk. Ms. Cook, however, was less than pleased with little Johnny's continuing tardiness. She folded her arms across her chest, staring the little boy down.

"This is the fourth time you've been late to class *this week*, Johnny."

"I know, Ms. Cook."

"And do you know what that means?"

"Yes, ma'am."

"What? *What* does it mean, Johnny?"

"That today's Thursday."

Lesson on Governance

A Little Johnny Story

Ms. Cook was teaching her class about the American system of government. At the end of class, she gave her students a homework assignment; they each had to go home and ask their parents to explain what government is in their own words.

As soon as little Johnny got home he went to his father's study and asked his dad a simple question. "Dad, what's the government?"

"Well, son, look at it like this, okay? I'm the President, your mom is Congress, our maid is the workforce, you're the People, and your baby sister is the future."

"I still don't get it."

"Well, why don't you sleep on it tonight, then? Maybe you'll understand it better in the morning."

"Okay, dad."

Johnny went to sleep that night but woke up to the sound of his baby sister crying down the hall. Johnny got up and walked down to his sister's room. After opening the door he walked over to her crib where he soon discovered she'd used the bathroom and needed a fresh diaper. Johnny then made his way to his parents' room, but he stopped. Instead of opening the door he looked through the keyhole to make sure they were asleep. His mom was there, in bed and snoring away, but his dad was nowhere to be seen. Now, Johnny instead went to the maid's room. When he peeped through her keyhole, however, he discovered his dad having sex with the maid.

And then it all made perfect sense.

The next day at school, Ms. Cook asked if any of her students had figured out what the government was. So proud he couldn't wait, Johnny stood up as he raised his hand.

"Yes, Johnny?"

"I understand the government perfectly, Ms. Cook."

"Well then, Johnny, please share with the rest of the class."

"Well, class, you see—the President is fucking the workforce, Congress is fast asleep, nobody cares about the People, and the future is full of shit!"

Ms. Cook fainted.

Sleepy Little Judy

A Little Johnny Story

It was no secret that Little Judy was not the best student in Sunday school. She rarely paid any attention to her lessons, preferring instead to sleep through class. One day Mrs. Anderson decided she ought to try to do something to get Judy more engaged in class. So, while Judy was asleep Mrs. Anderson called on her to answer a question.

"Tell me, Judy—who created the Universe?"

When Judy failed to respond, little Johnny, seated right behind her, took the pin holding a ribbon to his shirt and poked her in the butt.

"GOD ALMIGHTY!" Judy shouted as she came awake with a start.

"Very good, Judy, you're absolutely right." Mrs. Anderson applauded with a smile. Grumpily, Judy eventually dozed back off. Not long after, Mrs. Anderson saw this and so again she called on Judy.

"Judy, who is our Lord and Savior?" Once again, however, Judy was too deep in her sleep to hear the question. Thus, once again, Johnny came to the rescue, sticking her in the butt with his pin once more.

"JESUS CHRIST!" Judy screamed as she woke up once again.

"Good job, Judy, I'm proud of you." The teacher congratulated before continuing on with her lesson as Judy yet again settled down and fell back into her sleepy ways. Eventually, however, Mrs. Anderson again noticed her sleeping and decided this time she'd give the girl a more difficult question.

"Judy, can you tell me what Eve said to Adam after giving birth to her twenty-third child?"

Judy, however, remained asleep, and so again Johnny stabbed her with his pin. This time Judy jumped to her feet and screamed out.

"I SWEAR TO GOD IF YOU STICK THAT FUCKING THING IN ME ONE MORE TIME I'LL BREAK IT IN HALF AND SHOVE IT STRAIGHT UP YOUR ASS!"

Mrs. Anderson fainted.

The Runaround

A Little Johnny Story

Little Johnny was walking home from school one day when a police car pulled up next to him, stopping just shy of driving onto the sidewalk itself.

"Afternoon, son!" One of the cops shouted by way of greeting as he stepped out of his patrol car.

"Afternoon, Officer." Johnny greeted.

"You on your way home from school?"

"Yes, sir."

"Did you learn anything good today?"

"Not really."

"Son, where do you live?" The second cop asked.

"With my parents."

"And where do your parents live?"

"With me." Johnny answered truthfully.

"And where do all of you live?"

"Together."

The first cop chuckled. "Son, where's your house?"

"Next to my neighbor's house."

"And where is your neighbor's house?"

"Officer, sir, you just wouldn't believe me if I told you."

"Try me."

"It's next to our house."

The Sex Lesson

A Little Johnny Story

Little Johnny came home from school one day and went into the living room where his parents were watching television.

"Dad, what's sex?"

His dad thought for a moment before answering him. "Well, Johnny, I guess you're old enough now that you can know." And then he turned and instructed his wife to get undressed while he did the same thing. "Now, Johnny, you see that hole on ol' ma there?"

"Yes, sir."

"Well, watch your ol' pa here."

And so Johnny watched with fascination while his mom and dad had sex. Shortly afterwards, Little Jill came into the room and found herself shocked by what she was seeing.

"Johnny, Johnny, what are they doing?!"

"Jill, that there's what you call sex." Johnny explained proudly.

"Sex?"

"Yup."

"What's sex?"

Johnny, in turn, also took off his clothes. "Well, you see that hole on ol' Pa there?"

"Yeah?"

"Well watch little Johnny here!"

Time Out

A Little Johnny Story

One afternoon after school little Johnny was alone in the living room, playing with his giant toy school bus. As the bus driver, it was his responsibility to go along his route and get the good folks of town on their way.

Johnny would drive a bit and then he'd stop.

"All you motherfuckers that want to get on, get on! All you motherfuckers that want to get off, get off!"

His mother was in the kitchen when she overheard this, but surely she couldn't have heard him right. She paused to listen, and a minute or two later her little Johnny again reached his next stop.

"All you motherfuckers that want to get on, get on! All you motherfuckers that want to get off, get off!"

His mother came running into the living room, tossing her kitchen towel to the floor. She then jerked Johnny from the floor, swatted him once on the butt and sent him to his bedroom, telling him not to come out until he could learn to play right and be nice.

Thirty minutes later Johnny came into the kitchen, red-eyed and apologetic. He apologized to his mom for being so mean to the people on his route and assured her that he'd learned his lesson. Pleased, she sent him on to play with his bus once again. She listened in, and a few minutes later Johnny seemed to have reached his next stop.

"All of you nice people who want to get on, please get on. All of you nice people who want to get off, please get off."

His mother smiled.

"And for all of you motherfuckers who want to know why I'm so damn late, ask the bitch in the kitchen!"

Urinate

A Little Johnny Story

Little Johnny was at school one morning when he suddenly had to use the restroom. Standing up, Johnny raised his hand and patiently waited until his teacher called his name.

"Ms. Cook," He explained hurriedly. "I *really* have to go piss!"

"Johnny!" Ms. Cook chided him sternly. "That is *not* the appropriate word for a young gentleman to use. The proper word is 'urinate'."

"Ms. Cook—"

"Please use the word 'urinate' correctly in a sentence and I'll allow you to go."

Johnny thought for but a second before providing his response. "Well, Ms. Cook, you're an eight but if your tits were a little bigger you'd be a ten."

Adult Jokes

A Man's First Time

Even after all of these years I still remember my first experience with a condom. I was about sixteen or so when it happened.

I'd gone in to buy a pack of condoms at our local pharmacy: my parents were out of town for the weekend and my girlfriend of one year was planning to come over and spend the night, just the two of us. When I walk into the store, however, the first thing I notice—almost *immediately*—is that there's a beautiful, plump redheaded woman working the register. I mean, I can immediately feel myself getting excited. I go up to ask for my condoms but my words just ramble out, my tongue tripping over itself. It was, looking back, pretty obvious that I was new at this. And she could see it. In a soft, gentle voice she asked me if I knew how to use one. I shook my head, opting for honesty. "No, this is my first time."

She pulled a condom out of its wrapper and slipped it over her thumb in an attempt to demonstrate to me how it should be done. She cautioned me to make sure it was on tight and that it was secure. Apparently I still looked confused, however, because soon she stopped and began looking around the store to make sure that it was empty.

It was.

"Just a minute." She said before walking to the front door, where she then turned the lock and made sure it could not be opened. She then came back, took my hand, and led me to the back storage room.

Once there she then unbuttoned her blouse and unhooked her bra, throwing both of them to the floor.

"Does this excite you?" She asked. I was so taken aback that all I could do was nod my head. She smiled, took off her pants and her panties and then helped me to undress as well. Once done she told me it was time for me to slip the condom on. I had to do it myself, she explained, as I needed to learn. So I'd done exactly what she taught me. She then had me lie down on the desk and after that she sat down on top of me and within just moments I was deep inside of her.

It was the best thing I'd ever felt. Unfortunately, it was also so very wonderful that in just a couple of minutes I'd lost all control of myself.

KAABOOM!

And just like that I was done.

She looked at me with a bit of a frown. "That was good, but did you put that condom on?"

"Sure did!" I exclaimed with a smile, holding up my hand to show her the condom on my thumb, just like she'd showed me.

She fainted.

Blueberry Hill

As the school's bell rang to signal the start of classes that morning, Principal Jones found himself standing outside the front doors, waiting for a handful of his students who had yet to show up for school.

After several long, silent minutes the first missing student came hopping up, trying to put his shoe on his foot.

"Freddy." Principal Jones greeted. "Where've you been this morning?"

"Sorry, Mr. Jones," Freddy apologized. "I got distracted on top of Blueberry Hill."

Mr. Jones frowned momentarily. He'd lived in these parts all his life and he'd never before heard of Blueberry Hill. Eventually, he waved Freddy on, instructing him to get to class. Blueberry Hill, he decided, must be some new kid thing.

A few minutes later another teenager came running along, stopping just long enough to buckle his belt.

"Jimmy." Mr. Jones said by way of greeting. "Where've you been, son?"

"Sorry, Mr. Jones—I got distracted on top of Blueberry Hill."

There was that mysterious Blueberry Hill again. What was all of this about? He shook his head, waving Jimmy onwards to class.

Minutes more passed before a third boy came running up, makeup smeared all over his face as he, too, paused to buckle his belt.

"Donnie."

"Mr. Jones."

"Where've you been?"

"Sorry, Mr. Jones—I got distracted on top of Blueberry Hill."

"Son, I think you got more than just a *little* distracted."

"I—yes, sir."

"Well, go on, then, get to class."

"Yes, sir."

"Oh, and Donnie?"

"Yes, sir?"

"Stop and check into the bathroom first, get that mess on your face cleaned up."

"I will, Mr. Jones."

And so Mr. Jones turned back around, waiting for any other wayward students who might be straggling behind.

Five minutes later another student, this time a teenage girl with makeup smeared all over her face came walking up, swaggering and full of bounce even as she struggled to get her top on properly.

"Joy."

"Hello there, Mr. Jones."

"Where've you been—wait, let me guess." He paused for dramatic effect. "You got distracted on top of Blueberry Hill."

"Oh, Mr. Jones, you're so funny." Joy laughed. "I wasn't on top of Blueberry Hill."

"Well, that's a rel—"

"I *am* Blueberry Hill."

Jack & Jill

Jack and Jill went up the hill,

So Jack could lick her candy.

But Jack got a shock and a mouthful of cock,

Because Jill's original name was Randy.

Mommy's Sponge

One day little Billy really had to use the bathroom. He was in such a hurry that he forgot to stop and knock on the bathroom door before walking in. Thus, when he opened the door he came face-to-face with his mother, naked and dripping wet from the shower she'd just taken. For several moments Billy just stood there, ashamed and afraid he might be in trouble. His mother, on the other hand, was nervous, as she was afraid she might have to have the sex talk a *lot* sooner than planned. However, soon enough curiosity overtook the little boy. He pointed towards his mother's legs.

"Mommy, what's that?"

It took his mother a moment to realize what her little boy meant, but eventually it dawned on her that he didn't recognize the mass between her legs as hair, and so she just might get away without ruining her son's innocence yet.

"Oh, that." She answered. "That's just Mommy's sponge. Now, go play with your toys while I get dressed and then you can come potty."

"Okay mommy." Little Billy responded, and off he went.

A few weeks passed and once again Little Billy found himself in sudden need to use the bathroom, and once again he forgot to knock on the bathroom door before walking in. Again he found himself walking in on his naked mother following a shower.

"Billy!" She screamed helplessly. "How many times do we have to tell you to knock on the door first?!"

"I'm sorry mommy I just *really* had to use the bathroom."

"I understand honey, bu—"

"Mommy?"

"What, Billy?"

"Where's your sponge?"

"I—oh." And then she remembered she'd shaven herself days prior as a surprise for her husband, and now she needed a new answer to placate her son. So it was that she decided to go with an easy answer. "I'm sorry, Billy, Mommy lost it."

"Oh, okay. Don't worry, Mommy, I'll help you find it."

"Okay, honey." She laughed, confident once more in her success. "Go play while mommy gets dressed and then you can come potty."

"'Okay, mommy."

A few more days passed and, to his mother's relief, Billy had no more incidents involving his walking in on her in the bathroom.

And then one sunny afternoon she found herself in the kitchen preparing dinner when little Billy ran in, out of breath and looking unusually excited.

"Mommy, Mommy, I found it! I found it!"

"You found what, Billy?"

"Your sponge! I found your sponge!"

"My sponge?"

"Yeah! You know, the one you had between your legs?"

"Oh, yeah, I remember." She laughed, having nearly forgotten the incident altogether. "I—so you found it?"

"I did! I did!"

"Okay—erm—where is it?"

"That blonde lady across the street has it and she's washing Daddy's face with it right now!"

Racing Pedophiles

Question: Why do pedophiles never compete in races?

Answer: Because they always come in a little behind.

The Great Penis Study

Back in the 1990s Great Britain commissioned a study to determine why the head of a man's penis is wider than the shaft. The study took over two years and cost over £1.2 million. In the end, the study concluded that the reason the head of a man's penis is so much larger is because it provides the man with more pleasure during sex, as the increased size can hold more nerve endings.

After these results were published France decided to conduct their own study on the subject; they were absolutely convinced that the British were wrong. After three years of study and a cost of €2 million the French scientists concluded that the British were indeed wrong. The reason for the extra size of the penis's head, the French declared, was to give the man's partner more pleasure during sex—for obvious reasons, of course.

Upon release of this study, the United States government decided that both of America's allies were incorrect. They were likely overthinking the subject, as one leading American official explained. As a way of settling the debate once and for all, the

U.S. commissioned its own study. After nearly three hours of arduous, scientific research and at a cost of an astounding $75 (the cost for three cases of beer), the Americans released their conclusion. Their scientists had discovered that the head of the penis was wider than the shaft to prevent the man's hand from flying off of the end of the shaft and hitting him in the forehead.

The Pill

Mary was Dr. Kevin's final patient of the day. When she walked in, she sat down on the exam table and so Dr. Kevin asked her what was going on.

"Well, Doc, my husband—I love him dearly, you know? We've been married almost twenty-five years now."

"Wow, that—that's a long time."

"Yeah, and I'd not trade it for anything."

"So, what's the problem?"

"He's lost it."

"It?"

"Yeah. He can't keep it up anymore and so now our sex life is practically extinct."

"Oh, I see."

"We've tried everything we can think of but nothing seems to work. We've tried natural remedies, home remedies, Viagra—*everything*!"

"I understand."

"Please, we're desperate. Is there *anything* you can do for him?"

"Well, I do have a new, experimental pill, but it's really, *really* strong. It might be too much."

"We'll try it."

"Okay, give me a minute here."

And a moment later Dr. Kevin handed Mary a small bottle of several pills, instructing her that he was giving her a one week's supply and that her husband should take one pill one time a day.

A month later, Mary returned. "Dr. Kevin, that pill worked great and the effects lasted a few weeks after he ran out, but now it's worn off."

"Okay, then, we'll increase his dosage." And so he gave her a larger bottle with a two week's supply. This time, he instructed her to have her husband take two pills twice a day. Mary thanked him and then she left.

Another two months passed before Mary returned. "Dr. Kevin, it worked better this time but it still ended up wearing off."

"Okay, then, it's time to get drastic." And this time Dr. Kevin gave her two of the largest bottles of pills Mary had ever seen, and inside were some of the largest pills she'd ever seen.

"Have him take three of these, three times a day, for three months, and it should fix his problem once and for all."

"Thank you, Dr. Kevin."

And so Mary left.

Two weeks later Dr. Kevin was preparing to close up his office and go home that night when Mary's son, little Billy, came rushing in, red-faced and breathless.

"Billy, what's wrong, son?"

"I-I'm sorry Doc—ran—fast as I could. I—your help."

"Calm down, Billy, and tell me what's going on."

"No. I need—I need you to come with me, now."

"Billy, I need you to calm down first—"

"No time—it's an emergency—"

"I understand that, son, but I can't help anyone if I don't know what's going on."

"F-fine. My—" Billy paused to catch his breath. "My mom came and got those big pills from you for my dad because he sucks in bed."

"Oh yeah, I remember. How—is everything okay?"

"Well, mom kept giving him the pills just like you'd instructed, but it wasn't having an effect yet, so after the first night she got desperate."

"Billy, what did your mom do?"

"She crushed all the pills up and put them into dad's spaghetti, all at once."

"Oh no, please say you're joking—"

"And now mom's dead, Sarah's pregnant, dad's on the roof going 'here kitty kitty' and my butt hurts!"

The Three Phases of Life

One night while the family was eating dinner Gary asks his father a question that's been burning in his mind for several days.

"Dad, how many kinds of boobs are there?"

Taken aback, his father is quiet for several minutes while he considers how best to answer his son's question. Eventually, though, he comes up with what he feels is an adequate answer.

"Well, son, during her life a woman goes through three phases with her breasts. Now, in her twenties they're like melons—round and firm. In her thirties and forties they become more like pears; still nice but now they hang a bit. After a woman hits the age of fifty, however, they become like onions."

"Onions, dad?" Gary asks in disbelief.

"That's right."

"Why onions?"

"Because, whenever you see them they make you cry."

Gary's mother and sister, meanwhile, become utterly annoyed by what Gary's just learned from his father. Deciding turnabout's fair play, Sally turns to her mother.

"Momma, how many kinds of penises are there?"

Her mother doesn't even hesitate.

"Well, dear, men also go through three phases with their penises during the course of their lives. In his twenties a man's penis is like an Oak Tree—mighty, strong, and hard. In his thirties and forties it becomes more like a Birch Tree; flexible but reliable. After a man hits fifty, however, it becomes just like a Christmas Tree."

"A Christmas Tree?" Sally asks with a laugh.

"That's right, honey. It's dead from the root up and the balls are just for decoration."

The Trucker's Son

Old man Harold was a retired minister enjoying his twilight years in his small hometown. Everyone knew him and everyone loved and respected him. Also serving as an old country doctor, he'd either delivered or married nearly everyone in town.

One bright, spring morning he stepped outside to enjoy the smell of the flowers blooming in his front yard and the weather of such a perfect April day. However, while he was outside Harold noticed quite an unusual sight.

Across the street a neighbor boy he recognized as little Mike was sitting on the bottom step of his porch, holding a bag of M&Ms in one hand and the family's old cat in the other. While Harold watched, the boy would bite the cat, pop one or two M&Ms into his mouth, and then move up a step. He'd then wait a minute or two and repeat the process. Finally, at long last, curiosity got the better of old Harold and so he walked himself across the street.

"Hello, Mike." Harold greeted as the boy moved up to the next step in line.

"Hello, Mr. Harold, sir. How are you today?"

"I'm doing well, son, how are you?"

"'I'm doing pretty well too, sir, thank you for asking."

"Son, I couldn't help but notice what you're doing from my front lawn. May I ask what it is—what you're doing?"

"Well, Mr. Harold, you know my daddy's a truck driver."

"Yes, I'm aware of that."

"Well, when I grow up I want to be just like my daddy."

"That's all well and good, Mike, but what does that have to do with anything?"

"Well, I'm practicing being a truck driver, you see?"

"Oh?"

"Yes sir. I'm eating pussy, popping pills, and moving on up!"

True Stories

Author's Note

I would like to take a moment and let everyone who's made it this deep into *Duct Tape & Cheeseburgers* know a highly important fact. For the most part I have retained the names of those involved, unless I decide it's prudent or safer to change their names. If you're someone mentioned in the coming stories—sorry, if I have to suffer these events being outed then so do you.

The following stories are absolutely true. They are based off of my memories and old journal entries and retold in my own words.

As a writer I pride myself most of all on being honest and real. When writing fiction, even if it's Science Fiction or Fantasy, my words show the reader the true realities of life, both the good and the bad. Life has its good days but it's not always rainbows and unicorns. Some days are gritty, grimy, and hard. Some days we see humanity at its best and others at its lowest. As such the following stories have not been altered in any way but rather have been written and published exactly as they happened—as I warned on one of my first five pages, this book is not intended for anyone under the age of 16. So please, keep that fact in mind as you proceed into the next section of this book.

Smell Before You Drink

A True Story

"Look before you leap." This adage is, in all likelihood, as old as the Human species itself. It's pretty self-explanatory, right? I mean, the meaning of this proverb is that before you act you should first stop and consider all possible consequences. Again, rather straight forward, huh?

Yeah—not so much. Apparently, there *are* those out there who don't always remember this sage advice. I speak, of course, from experience. So, I'm here to introduce a new concept, a more modern approach, if you will.

Smell before you drink.

This is perhaps one of my most vivid memories from my teenage years. The year is 2002, the first summer after the terror attacks of September 11. I'd been living with my father (Charles) and stepmother (Vicky) in the small, backwoods town of Black Rock, Arkansas for now on about nineteen or twenty months. Now, moving from a city life in nearby Trumann to the more countrified style-of-living in Black Rock was a bit of a culture shock for me. From a home in the projects to living on nearly sixty acres of open land with but a single house or two in sight and being able to see the stars at night—well, that's a hell of a change, right?

Likewise, it certainly had to have been an equally difficult change for Charles and Vicky. To go from living alone to having a teenager in the midst of puberty among them—I often wonder how any of us survived. Now, my dad wasn't the best parent, nor was he the sharpest. His style of parenting was "Yes, Sir." "No, sir." "I'm your father and you'll respect me for it." "Do what I say when I say it." I was more "How about you ask nicely?" and "Respect is earned, not given." (I still have a bruise from the first three times I told him that last bit) He'd take things at face value and given how intelligent I was, even at fourteen years of age, I learned nearly immediately how to manipulate him, how to slide things by him without him catching on and simultaneously letting him retain his delusions of control. He was always easy to fool. Want proof? I've always been a bookworm. I'm a nerd; I have been all my life. I can quote a hundred books as easily as I can catch a fish. I've always loved reading. I've always loved writing. When I got my first F after moving in (in the span of three months I'd moved from Trumann to Paragould, then to Harrisburg, back to

Trumann, and then finally to Black Rock, and each time meant a different school. Thus, when I reached Black Rock I'd given up on academics for several months before I rediscovered my motivation), he grounded me. To my bedroom. Where all of my books and notebooks were. To my bedroom, with all of my pens and pencils. Talk about a vacation, right?

Wrong.

See, as dull as Charles was, Vicky was as sharp. From day one that redhead knew me as well as I did. She caught on immediately. Suddenly, getting grounded meant spending the day outside, away from the house, exploring sixty acres in the hot summer sun and the frigid winter winds. (Of course, I was basically raised on the St. Francis River so I'm as equally at home in the woods as I am in a library. Yeah, grounding went out of style PDQ.)

One of the things Vicky caught onto rather quickly is that Mountain Dew made me hyper. Not talkative hyper but a chipmunk-drinking-Red Bull-infused coffee-after-snorting-cocaine-hyper. Yeah, it was that bad. Naturally, can you guess what I was *never* allowed to drink?

Yup, you guessed it.

So, here we are. Summer of 2002. I come out of my bedroom after some special Kenny time (otherwise known as masturbating to the Penthouse I'd secretly kidnapped from Charles's collection he *thought* he'd hidden in the top shelf of the bathroom). It's hot, I'm thirsty—and I'm alone. We lived in a trailer sitting atop a hill and I was the only soul aboard.

Nice.

And then I notice it. The sweet beverage I so longed for. A Mountain Dew. Sitting on the counter unwatched and untended.

Great.

And then I notice something else; it's a 2-liter.

Better.

And it's full.

AWESOME!

I check every room and even shout out a few times to make absolutely sure it's safe. I mean, I'd seen cop shows before—I knew how sting operations worked. *So* not gonna be that guy.

I get to the kitchen and as I approach the nectar of the gods I look outside and I see that the truck's gone. Charles is too far away to stop me. And then I notice Vicky standing way out in the driveway talking to her friend, Kay, and I realize that baby, the light is green.

Yeah!

I open the bottle and pause, admiring the deliciousness about to grace my throat. At this point virgin me decided even sex couldn't possibly be exhilarating (Okay, yes, that analysis was wrong but cut me some slack—I wouldn't figure that out for another seven years). Christmas had come early, boys!

Right?

Yeah, no. My elation evaporated as quickly as my pride. Heaven became hell and my dream had faded into a nightmare.

Too late I learned the truth.

I'd been tricked. Bamboozled. Lied to. Fooled. Abused.

It wasn't Mountain Dew.

It was fool's gold.

It was Dawn dish soap.

Some cruel, desperate housewife who shall remain forevermore nameless (my stepmother) had allowed herself to run out of dish soap and so had borrowed some from next door, and to transport her ill-gotten booty she'd chosen a previously-empty Mountain Dew 2-liter bottle.

And she'd left it out.

The hook had inadvertently been baited and like the fat catfish I am I bit down and got caught—hook, line, and sinker.

Five minutes later I've got my head upside down under the faucet of the kitchen sink when I hear the front door open. Realizing I'm no longer alone I stand up, suds and bubbles covering my face while water is drenching my entire front. I glare at this redheaded she-devil with the hatred of a million suns, and she doesn't yell. She doesn't scream. She doesn't even laugh.

She smirks. "Well, guess you won't do that again, will you, Bubbles?"

And now I'm no longer angry, no longer irked. I'm embarrassed. I shake my head, my only solitude being that this day couldn't get any worse.

Right?

Yeah—WRONG!

She then goes to my bedroom while I sop my face and comes back with the stolen magazine that had brought me so much pleasure, pausing just long enough to ask me to remind her to kick my dad's butt for leaving his adult material in such an obvious place.

I can't just go quietly after this, can I? I've been thoroughly embarrassed and I need to get my revenge.

"I'd sleep with my eyes open if I was you, woman." I barked. "Your ass is mine."

She shook her head, surprising me—I should have lost teeth for that. I could occasionally get away with adult language in front of her—she wasn't as strict as Charles, but this, a threat? I was momentarily pleased.

"Go clean up your bedroom."

Five minutes later I come out, my sheets and comforter in my hands.

"Is the washer empty?" I asked. After all, my special Kenny fun times earlier that afternoon had left their mark.

"Don't worry about it—put those back on your bed."

I pause, unsure how to tell my stepmother that a blast of a million little Kenny soldiers had made their charge only to splatter lifeless against the enemy. And then, she looks up, catches my eyes, and as if my day wasn't bad enough—

"Don't worry son—I don't think that little worm made *that* much of a mess."

She should've just punched me.

The Culinary Misfit

A True Story

The first several months of 2006 were chaotic and confusing for me. My senior year of high school's conclusion had been quite the ride. My best friend, Jared, and I had gotten into a fight at school and we'd been suspended. On the first day of my suspension from school I receive a visit from a United States Marine; he was a recruiter, to be precise. He explained I'd made a 79 on my ASVAB. He further explained that the highest score possible was a 99 and that the average for the state of Arkansas at the time was a 30. As he put it, this basically meant I could have any job, any station, and any security clearance with the USMC that my heart desired.

Unfortunately, being well over 250 pounds and suffering from gout tends to stop any military career cold in its track.

So, when I graduated that May, I had no real plan for my future aside from get away from home. My father and I are as different as water and fire and we never really saw eye-to-eye. So, with the help of my neighbor and friend (and future one-time girlfriend) Samantha, I loaded up everything I owned and moved in with my mother, her boyfriend, and his daughter. However, I still had no plan for my future, no job, and I suffered from extreme insomnia.

Late one night (or early one morning) I saw an infomercial for the Job Corps program. I recognized it because a year or two before that night my mom's boyfriend, Tim, had told me of his time spent in Job Corp up in Detroit. So, I looked into it, having to travel from Jonesboro, Arkansas to Batesville, Arkansas. However, we found out I qualified perfectly and so I got to choose from the three job corps centers Arkansas hosted: Cass (outside of Ozark), Little Rock, and Ouachita (in Royal, near Hot Springs). In my mind, I literally processed it like this: fuck Little Rock and its gang-infested sewers. I'm hot enough in north Arkansas so forget the southern part of the state. The mountains are beautiful and cooler, so I'll take Cass.

So, I arrived at Cass on August 1, 2006 just after 10:30 that night (I travelled from Jonesboro to Memphis, Tennessee, to Little Rock, Arkansas, and then to Cass that day via Greyhound and that final bus had run extremely late), just three months or so after graduating high school. Now, for those who don't know or aren't familiar with the Job Corps program—I like to call it poor man's college, but that really isn't an accurate descriptor. It's a vocational program started back during the Great Depression to teach financially-challenged young adults and teenagers vital life skills so that they can be productive members of society. Cass offered nine vocational trades in addition to GED/High School Diploma and driver's education/licensing for those who needed it (This is how I actually got my first driver's permit and, later, driver's license). Our nine trades on center at the time were Culinary Arts, Business & Office Technologies, Brick Masonry, Painting, Carpentry, Welding, Concrete Masonry, Facilities Maintenance, and Heavy Machinery Operations. I myself graduated from both Culinary Arts and Business & Office Technologies, and I also spent some time in Carpentry.

Now, when you first arrive on-center you spend your first several weeks in orientation, getting settled in and used to life on center (Ours was a live-in center that operated 24/7). Once the orientation period was over it was time to select our desired trade(s). We had a three-day period we called OEP: Occupational Exploration Program. Basically, to put it simply, we'd spend one day in a trade to see what it was like, much like test-driving a car before buying it. Afterwards, we could try a different trade before making our decision. Now, it was still possible to change trades after making that final decision, but it was a lengthy, drawn out process that involved significant paperwork.

Now, I won't lie: OEP seems exciting, but a lot of times it sucked. You were the new kid, after all, and there was so much ritualistic hazing that went into (as some of the senior students called it) making the rookies earn their stripes. My OEP was no exception—I fell for the plastic welding rod gag while OEPing in Carpentry.

Now, those who know me that if there's one thing I hate it's a bully. Being a bully survivor myself, I despised it and stood up to it anywhere I saw it. However, Cass forced me to grow up. I still fought bullying wherever I found it, but things stopped being so black-and-white for me. My approach changed and I realized that, sometimes, there are people who are so stupid, who don't *try* to learn, or else just don't use their brain, that they bring a lot of the trouble and grief they get on themselves.

During my nineteen months at Cass there was no one who did this quite so well as the boy we called Lieutenant Dan. Where—or how—he got his nickname I have no idea. All I know about him now, thirteen years later, is that his name was Murphy but I can't recall if it was his first or last name. To everyone, even the staff, his name was Lt. Dan (But from here on we'll just call him Dan).

Dan was the ultimate misfit. At first I tried to be nice and friendly with; after all, I myself knew what it was like to be the weird one with no friends. However, those efforts quickly met their demise. He was a sixteen year-old (Cass admitted students between the ages of 16 – 24) mouthy little bastard who thought so very highly of himself. To ask him, no one was smarter, more experienced, stronger, or better.

Dan washed out of every trade that would take him. He'd mess the work up, cause accidents, forget to use proper safety equipment, or else be too lazy to do the work. I mean, the man made Jar Jar Binks look elegant, graceful, and desirable.

Finally, however, the day came when there was only one trade he'd *not* washed out of, the trade that was now his final chance to avoid being expelled and sent home.

Culinary Arts.

Never, in a million years, would I have believed he'd have the audacity to try out with us. Our kitchen wasn't just for training—the students in the Culinary program were the center's cooks. We were the ones responsible for cooking breakfast, lunch, and dinner day in and day out. We cooked meals for three hundred-plus people three times a day, without fail. It's a demanding, demeaning, rough experience that even I had trouble surviving at times.

When I earned my blue apron (we had three apron colors: white for newbies, red for intermediate, and blue for senior student cooks/student shift leaders. Staff cooks wore green aprons) I was excited and I was proud. On my first day as a senior student cook I was assigned to rearrange and inventory our dry stock room. Knowing this would be a ten or eleven-hour job, I brought my radio with me to play some music (those who know me know I do my best work when I have music to listen to). Barely an hour after starting one of my best friends, Jesse Diffee, comes back to me and kills my radio before taking me towards the back corner of the room.

"Listen, Ken, Red's done gone and done it now." To clarify, Red was the name we called our red-haired Culinary instructor.

"What's he done?"

"We've got Lieutenant Dan today."

I laughed. He was joking, right? Red was a hell of a man willing to give anyone a fair chance, but even he knew Murphy would be eaten alive in our kitchens, especially since anyone trying out with us was put on KP duty. Yes, I know it sounds weird to some that your first days of Culinary Arts be spent on Kitchen Patrol doing dishes, but something I always respected about our instructor was that Red believed a cook or chef needed to have the utmost respect for the men and women who washed dishes. I agreed.

"No." I laughed again. "Stop messing with me."

"I'm not: he's OEPing with us today."

I look out the door and sure enough I see this poor boy in his brown OEP uniform collecting a pair of dirty utensils from the floor.

"For fuck's sake."

"Listen, Colonel and I are about to pull a fast one on him."

"Come again?"

"Yeah, we're going to send him back here to find some dehydrated water. I—"

"Come on, Diffee, even Dan's not *that* stupid."

"I'm telling you this because I know you're a goody-goody, so please, when he comes back here don't take pity and ruin it for us."

I laugh again. "Look, if Dan's stupid enough to fall for this one he *deserves* it."

"That's what I want to hear."

And so Diffee disappears back into the main kitchen, leaving me alone with my music once more. A few minutes later, per Diffee's words, Murphy's little self comes into Dry Storage and starts randomly rummaging through the shelves.

I ignore him. Surely he's not looking for dehydrated water. Surely not. I mean—*no one's* that stupid, right?

Right?

Yeah—wrong. So, so wrong.

Maybe ten minutes pass before the boy has this bright idea to come to me and ask for my help.

"Ken, that dehydrated water—do you know where it's at?"

I immediately join in. In my mind, I literally tell myself *'Fuck being nice, this kid needs to learn a lesson.'*

"I don't, actually; I only just got back here and got started with inventory."

"Oh, okay then. Do—do you know if it's in bottles or cans?"

"It's in boxes, actually, kinda like the milk cartons we got in school."

"Oh, okay then!"

"Yeah. Like I said, I know they're back here somewhere but I'm not quite sure myself. I wish I could help you more."

"No, that's plenty of help; I know I can find them now."

Yeah. Dan spent the next *two hours* searching the dry storage room top and bottom. At long last, unable to watch his bumbling foolishness anymore, one of our staff cooks, Ms. Brenda (we had two ladies named such, one nice, one not so nice—luckily for Murphy, this day we had the former) comes back there and explains how and why dehydrated water is an oxymoron and that the cooks had just pulled a practical joke on him.

I *almost* felt guilty at this point, not just because he looked so down but because Ms. Brenda gave me that "I'm disappointed; you should know better" look that old women seem so masterfully able to give. Still, I shrug it off: maybe this would be a lesson and he'd start thinking about things. Maybe he'd start using his brain some.

Were that it was to be. Alas, it was not, as I would soon discover.

Shortly after this, it was time for me to grab some grub and take my lunch break. When I exited the dry storage room I entered the main kitchen. I entered the giant walk-in freezer to grab something—I can't remember what—and upon opening I found Dan inside it, along with a mop, bucket, and "Wet Floor" sign. He'd been persuaded to mop the freezer, with it on and the door locked. I just shook my head and went about my lunch. Eventually he *had* to learn, right?

Wrong.

After lunch I came back in, preparing to go back to inventory, when a new sight stopped me dead in my tracks. Once again, it was Dan. Now out of the freezer, he was at the spice rack—or rather, what had *once* been our spice rack. At one point it had held dozens of bottles of our best spices, yet now it was mostly empty. Upon talking to him, I realized what was going on: one of our student cooks had persuaded this poor fool to *alphabetize* our spice rack. Now, for those who think that this isn't the worst thing possible—oh yes it is. See, our spices were arranged by potency, starting at the left with the weak, mild spices and ending with spices that only a dragon could handle on the far right.

I'd finally had enough. I grabbed the poor fool by his collar, lifted him up, and carried him seven-or-so feet to the walk-in freezer door where I then slammed his back into said door.

"You fucking kid! Wake up, grow up, and use your damn mind for once in your life!" I was quite fed up at this point. I let it *all* out. "You cry that people bully you and take advantage of you but you make it so laughably easy for them. You're assigned to KP today, that's *it!* If a student cook, even one with a blue apron, asks you to do something, you *don't,* because it's going to get you into fucking trouble, you pathetic little dunce!

Now get back to the washroom and don't leave again until your shift ends or I'll put my foot so far up your ass you can use my ingrown toenail (a constant health problem I suffered from during my time at Cass) as a toothpick!"

And for the rest of the day he did pretty well. Not great but he did acquit himself at times. That is, until I heard him smack-talking me behind my back. Yup, it was time the kid was put in his place. While he went to use the restroom I snuck into the washroom and disconnected a few parts so that he couldn't do his job properly. Lucky for me, after 2:30 the kitchens got incredibly slow for a few hours as we were between meals.

Sure enough, my plan worked. Dan came up to me later that afternoon to tell me that the hose had stopped working.

"Okay, we have to move quick, Mr. Murphy, because we have dinner rush coming soon and we're gonna need that hose."

"What do I do?"

"Run down to Facilities Maintenance before they close. Tell whoever you can find that we need a Model FU06LD Sky Hook with a Flaccid Willy Attachment and then hurry up and bring it back."

Looking so damn eager to please he turned and ran off.

Dan never returned to the kitchen and I had to have one of our newer cooks take over the dishes for the rest of the afternoon which meant the rest of my shift was spent in inventory and helping out as needed in the kitchen. So worth it, though, *especially* when I heard word that Dan refused to come over to Culinary, eventually deciding to stay in Welding, the (arguably) laziest trade on sight where 80% of the students spent time goofing off instead of applying their trade. It was also the only other trade that hadn't outright kicked him out.

And that's the end of the story, right?

Ha! Wrong!

That was 2007. Now fast-forward to 2014, seven years almost to the month. I found out one of my best friends, almost like a brother, really, had gone full-blown dark side. Raped one ex-girlfriend, molested a thirteen year-old. Yeah. And he was sending me nudes of random women I'd never met—except one of them I had. It was a girl I'd met a few times while at Cass. Recognizing her, I messaged her via Facebook and gave her the image, explaining where I'd received it.

Within a month we had become literal best friends. I'm serious—the connection we scared was—is—frightening. One weekend she came up to visit myself and another of our mutual friends, and I told her this very story. And then, when I'm done, she looks at me like I'd raped and murdered her favorite puppy in front of her.

"Kenneth Dewayne!"

"Yes, mom?" I ask out of habit—after all, though she'd been dead five years, I generally only got middle-named by my mother, and when it happened I always knew I was in trouble.

"That was *YOU?!*"

For fuck's sake. It was only now that I remembered two exceptionally-important facts. First, Lacey had been at Cass when this had happened. Second—she was a student in the Facilities Maintenance shop. She'd been there when he came asking for that sky hook.

Yup.

She lectured me. And she explained—without going into details—that her compatriots had utterly destroyed this kid to the point that he ran away in tears.

Now I felt horrible. For a moment. Then I remembered he'd brought most of his troubles on himself. Fuck regret. Regret's for lesser mortals.

To Japan

Late in 1995 Mom revealed to everyone that she was—once again—pregnant. Immediately, I wanted to be optimistic and excited, but I was cautious. I'd gotten excited before. I'd been *burned* before.

You see, of my mother's children I am the oldest, born on a dreary Saturday morning in 1988. Next was my sister, Alicia, in 1990. And then there was Anna in 1993. Now you see my quiet panic setting in. One boy (myself) versus three girls in the home, poor Kenny was just outnumbered all around. Sure, I had Pa, and as my grandfather spending *every* weekend with him and my grandmother was a much-needed reprieve from my conquest by estrogen, but that was only a couple of days a week, right? It was like I told my mom—I *needed* a baby brother. To be honest, every boy does. A young apprentice he can ~~corrupt~~ train and teach. A partner in crime. Shit rolls downhill and every boy needs a younger brother he can divert some of that to.

I still remember the day Mom came home with the ultrasound image. Alicia and Anna—six and three at that time, respectively—were excited: they were about to get another baby sister to dress up, play with, and love on, someone not mean and crass like their big brother (I acquitted myself well when it came to my God-given duty to make their lives a living hell). I was so upset, however, that I was in denial. Mom, of course, tried to explain to me that I was wrong. If it was a boy, she explained, we'd be able to see his pecker in the ultrasound.

I still remember my answer to that. "By Godzilla, woman! Maybe he's just hiding it; I know *I* wouldn't like some stranger taking weird-looking pictures of *my* pecker."

And then May 19 came, and Mom gave birth to her fourth living (and final) child. One month later she brings this pink bundle of skin home, calling her "Samantha" (It's important to note that Samantha was born two months early and was kept in the hospital for nearly a full month). Looking at this bundle of miniaturized humanity wrapped in a pink blanket, I could no longer deny the truth.

I was *angry.* I looked my mother straight in the eyes and I told her "You take it back right now and get your money back, and then get me a little brother!"

However, she only laughed. "I'm afraid that's not how it works, Kenny."

"Of course it is—you do it at Wal-Mart's all the time!"

However, Mom kept to her guns and I soon realized the truth: I'd be stuck with this new baby sister, right?

Wrong!

Kenneth Dewayne Simpson has never been one to give up. No joke, I don't know how to leave well-enough alone. Oh yes, I would get rid of this fourth woman in my household. This was no longer a battle to stop the flood of estrogen invading my life, it was war and I was ol' General Stonewall. Oh, yes. All I had to do was plan and bide my time, and once I got the chance, then—well, fix bayonets, gentlemen, because we gonna charge 'em! Know what I mean?

As luck would have it, I got my chance about four months later. As luck would have it, we were out of school one October day due to a teacher's in-service day, and so mom caught Samantha asleep in her crib and decided to take a shower. Oh yes, time to make my move.

While Alicia and Anna were next door playing with their friends, I snuck myself into mom's room, pulled Samantha out of the crib, and gently laid her into a great, whopping box that had held the T.V. my mom had just recently bought. I then grabbed some duct tape and taped the box shut. Once done, I then grabbed a book of stamps and a black magic marker, and proceeded to complete my task. Placing the stamps all over the box I then wrote "TO: JAPAN" and "WARNING: CONTENTS FRAGIL" on the top *and* the sides.

Now, I know what you're thinking. "You monster! How could you do such a thing!? Don't you love your sister?! How dare you?!"

Look, I didn't hate the poor runt, but cut a kid some slack, you know? I was desperate. And hey, I'm no monster—I made sure to punch a few dozen holes in the top of the box to make sure she could breath, and before taping the top I'd put some bottles, a can of formula, and a jug of water in the box with her. Why, I even made sure to put in some of her favorite toys. I'm not a complete monster, you know?

My task complete and mom still in the shower I pushed the box out onto the porch (no small feat for a boy of eight years) and then sat down on top of the box, patiently waiting for the mailman to come by.

About half an hour later it's getting about that time and then I hear the door open behind me as mom comes out onto the porch.

"Kenny, have you seen Samantha?"

"Samantha?" I ask, feigning ignorance. I'm so close to victory that I can *taste* it. I refuse to give in. Not now. "Samantha who? I don't know a Samantha, do you know a Samantha? What's a Samantha?"

And, because of course, little Samantha hears mom's voice and so she *immediately* begins to cry. Mom just looks at me and so I stare right back. "Woman, yo baby's in her crib crying! Go check on her!"

I wish I could say it totally worked, but no—no, it didn't. Mom grabs me straight up, a vertical lift, by the back of my shirt and drops me next to the box. She then rips the tape off of the box and—well, the gig's up.

She lights my poor butt up like it's the Fourth of July—at least *I* was seeing fireworks. She gets me with her hand, a flip flop, a belt, and a couple other objects I couldn't even recognize. By the time she's done I am beaten, battered, and in complete surrender; war over, right?

Ha! Yeah, no! My mother, once she's utterly murdered me, then waits a few hours to go for the kill shot. I mean, she goes straight for the heart.

She calls daddy.

No. Not *my* daddy. *Her* daddy. I can still remember as though it was yesterday. When he answers the phone she goes from angry to hurt like a master actor. She turns on the water factory, telling her dad about how his prized grandson tried mailing her baby off to Japan, how his minion had stuffed her into a box and taped it shut (completely leaving out the fact I'd put her stuff in there with her *and* put holes in the box, I might add). So then she hangs up the phone. And just like that, the tears are gone.

"Now you're in for it." She tells me before making me sit on the couch. Were this a movie, this would be the scene where you cue the Imperial March while zooming out and following Pa's old gold Chevy from his house across town all the way to our house.

Five minutes later I look up and see the truck that's usually my salvation pull up outside. I watch Pa get out and then I follow him as he comes up the door.

My goose is cooked. I know it. He comes in and Mom tells me to tell him what I'd done. So, thinking fast, I spin my story.

"Well, Pa, I've had a *heck* of a day." I explain. "Some stranger came in, put Sam in a box, and tried to mail her to Japan. *Japan*! Luckily I was here, though. I was trying to save her when mom got out of the shower and now Mom blames *me*! I was—"

"Kenny, don't lie to me." He cuts me off. "Tell me the truth."

And now I'm caught. With a heavy sigh I at last confess to my actions, explaining *why* I'd done it. Unlike Mom, however, I include my humanitarian efforts in keeping her safe and comfortable during transit.

Once finished I sit there, expecting *another* round of Beat the Kenny. However, he doesn't spank me. He doesn't yell, he doesn't scream. He just takes my hand in his and then proceeds to say the thirteen most devastating words I've ever heard in my life.

"I'm not mad at you, Kenny."

"You're not?"

"No, I'm just so disappointed in you."

Talk about murder. My hero, my idol, has just utterly destroyed my eight year-old mind. I wanted to beg him to spank me, to yell at me, cuss at me, berate me, beat me to a bloody pulp. Just *anything* but the line "I'm so disappointed in you."

I cried for a full week.

It's Going to Be Okay

Kids say the darndest things. This may just be an adage to some, but anyone who's ever spent any regular time in the presence of children knows that it is the gospel truth. I mean, you just never know what's going to come out of their mouths; taking them out in public can be much like playing a game of Russian Roulette. Perhaps no memory reminds me of this fact as much as this one from several years ago.

In late July of 2013 I travelled north with my girlfriend at the time, Genevra. We left from her home in Bartlett, Tennessee and drove up to Worcester, Massachusetts. While it was a vacation to me (I rarely got away from home at the time), we were actually going to help out a friend of hers as staff members of a two week-long Harry Potter-themed summer camp (Wiogoria School of Wonder & Wisdom—if you're in the area in late July and you have kids I fully advise adding it to their summer checklist). It was a load of fun and an experience I will *never* forget. I learned more than I'd ever thought possible and discovered myself in a way I could never have imagined.

However, it wasn't *all* fun and games. Genevra's three year-old daughter had developed a large cold sore on the inside of her bottom lip, and this poor kid was in such excruciating pain, *especially* when she'd drink or eat something. For nearly three or four days straight all she could do was scream and cry because of the pain—it really broke my heart, you know?

One night, her pain and the screaming and crying came to a head. At nearly three in the morning both Genevra and I had been up with this poor baby for over five hours straight. We'd exhausted everything in our collective arsenals to calm her down, to comfort her and make her feel better. I'd reached the limit of my patience and I knew Genevra—who usually had so much more patience than I did—wasn't too far behind.

Yet just as we reached the edge of that fathomless cliff, the crying and screaming suddenly stops. Just like that. It's like someone flipped a light switch. Genevra and I looked at each other, eyebrows raised in concerned confusion, but before either of us could speak or act, this wee thing of a child sat up, looked at her mother, looked at me, looked back at her mother, and then rested her gaze on the air mattress between us.

"Relax, you guys, just calm down, okay? It's going to be okay. I promise, it's gonna be just fine."

And then she collapses and she's suddenly as asleep as if she'd been asleep for hours.

I look at Genevra. "What just happened?"

"Isn't it obvious?" She asks, throwing herself back down. "We're both drunk and sharing a dream."

Kids say the darndest things, indeed.

The Man-Eater

I remember two things about October of 2012. It was almost as unseasonably warm as September of 2019. It was also the month I spent living with my step-brother.

To explain, in October of 2012 my step-brother's now-ex-wife came to pick me up in Monette and take me back to their house in Hoxie for a job fair. Now, for those unfamiliar with Northeast Arkansas, Hoxie is about 40 or 50 miles from Monette. Our initial plan was for me to spend two weeks there for both the job fair and to help them get their house cleaned and fixed up, among other things I shan't discuss. One of the few things I'm extremely good at, as most of my family knows, is cleaning up a messy house. So, I packed some clothes and also included some personal belongings to keep me occupied during my down-time. Among these personal effects was my R2-D2-themed XBOX 360.

Of course, as most of us can agree, no plan survives contact with the enemy. My two week stay turned into a five-week stay, from the last week of September to just a day or two before Halloween. A *lot* happened during those five weeks; work, drama, sex, video games—it was a rollercoaster. It was hot and sweaty and it was fun at times. However, the one thing I'll remember the most is what happened on my last Saturday night there, just four days or so before I came home.

That night my step-brother, Jason, was out of the house for the evening; on the side he performed as an amateur wrestler for a local independent promotion and their shows were on Saturday nights. His then-wife, Jennifer, had gone up to Black Rock (about fifteen miles north of Hoxie) to see her brother and sister-in-law. Jason's son, Devin, was gone for the night and so it was me at their house alone, with but their dog, cat, and her young kittens for company.

Of course, for me this was really no problem. Yes, their house was haunted. I knew this, even if they refused to acknowledge it. However, my step-brother's show was only a few blocks away, and though they didn't have internet I had plenty to occupy my time. I turned on my XBOX, popped in *Call of Duty: Modern Warfare 3* and played some survival mode.

I remember getting really into this particular match of survival. As such, I barely noticed that the kittens were making some weird noises in the back hallway. As my game continues their mother comes flying into the living room from the kitchen before disappearing into the hallway. Again, however, I barely even pay this any attention: I'm by myself and getting swarmed by enemy soldiers, you know? I have bigger fish to fry at this point.

Then the dog jumps down from my lap and also runs into the hallway, but again I give no care. Finally, however, I'm brought down and my match is over. And then, as I await my next match, I at last realize that the cat and her kittens are making some weird noises—noises they *should* not be making.

I get up and investigate what's happening. I expect maybe to find a kitten stuck in a shirt or the kittens playing and fighting, as kittens are so prone to do.

Were I so lucky.

I come into the hallway and I find the cat with a *snake* in her mouth. A living, breathing, slithering snake. I freeze and she just looks at me like "Oh, hi, fancy meeting you here."

And that damn snake, I swear on everything holy, looks up at me with a look of "Hiss, hiss, motherfucker."

Oh hell no! I turn and sprint out of the house, not stopping as I scoop my phone off of the couch. I mean, I literally almost knocked the doorframe down trying to escape this sudden death trap.

Once outside I call Jennifer and the moment she answers her phone I tell her that there is a giant snake in the house and I need someone to help me catch it (and by catch it I mean someone to come kill it for me).

"Kenny, this better not be a ploy to get me back there because you think the house is haunted and don't want to be there alone."

"First off," I responded. "Your house *is* haunted, and second, this snake is fucking *huge*! Now come save me!"

She mentions she's on her way and hangs up the phone. About ten minutes later a pair of cars and a truck pulls up and my step-brother and some of his buddies pile out. With reinforcement now in tow, I at last enter the house.

We tear that place apart but we don't find the snake. It has disappeared into thin air.

"How big was it, Kenny?" My step-brother asks.

"I'd estimate five or six feet long—he's big and grown."

"Do you know what kind?"

"Rattlesnake."

"You sure?"

"No doubts at all."

My sister-in-law shows up and she, too, joins in the hunt. However, we still can't find this thing.

Everyone gets ready to leave, convinced I'd made the story up while I was beginning to assume the cat had killed and eaten her prize.

And then we hit the jackpot.

As Jason and his friends head for the door Jennifer shouts out from their bedroom that she's found it. We all go in there and here I come face-to-face with my six-foot long rattlesnake assailant.

All five inches of it looking so small it almost looked like just a fat earthworm.

Oh, and it wasn't a rattlesnake.

It was a chicken snake.

What can I say? All snakes look the same when they're your major phobia.

Questions & Answers

This final section isn't necessarily humor-related, per se, but rather a chance for the various people I know (both in real life and those I know online) to ask me various questions and have them answered, honestly, in a manner that cannot be retracted or altered. So, feel free to read both the questions and my responses. Also, note that, as this is me at my realest, I'm not so much worried about grammar from this point on, so don't judge too harshly.

Question: What do you do when you suffer intense writer's block? (Asked by **Jaime Gray**)

Writer's Block. The two most dreaded words any writer will ever face. Well, the first thing I do is accept it: *every* writer will go through it at least once so there's no getting around that. It's also important to note that every writer is different. For as many people put pen to paper there are twice as many ways to overcome this dreaded disease. I myself often find that taking a break from writing can help. Video games are also a big help to me—especially if I can find a game that's similar to the story I'm writing. For example, the novel I'm currently working on is a fantasy *Game of Thrones/Elder Scrolls*-style world, so playing *Skyrim* has helped me get over writer's block with it several times. Writing fanfiction also helps me, particularly when I add elements from the novel I'm writing at that time—it's akin to approaching a problem from a different angle. However, perhaps nothing has helped me as much as my Circle. Having a Circle is something I'd encourage any writer, particularly one focusing on fiction, to have. To clarify, a Circle (as I mean it here) is a small group of trusted friends and confidants that the writer can ask to beta read their story, bounce ideas off of, and ask for advice when they reach a tough spot. My Circle is so vital to my writing because each person has different ideas and beliefs and, much like a fanfiction, it helps me see a problem from different angles, often allowing me to come up with an effective solution as well.

Question: What is your process for writing? Meaning—do you have vague idea of what you wanna write and just type as you go, or do you do a lot of brainstorming and outlining to get the frame of the story and *then* start? (Asked by **Chris Hale**)

Well, I do, but I don't. What I mean by that is that sometimes I just have an idea pop into my mind, form, and then I take off with it, adapting and evolving with the idea on the fly. It's one of my strengths, though it can also be a weakness. At times, however, I recognize that a book or story is going to be so expansive, so deep and complex, that I first force myself to draft an outline so that I can keep everything in order and straight, otherwise these stories will grow so large and so deep that I forget storyline material I want to add *and* this will also lead to various continuity errors. The first novel I wrote is a prime example of this: it was deep and complex, with a dozen various characters, but I just went with it on the fly. As a result, among other things, I had one character never be named and one character who had one name for half the book and a second name for the rest of the novel. So, these days it depends on the story and the depth I plan on going with it whether or not I just take off or plan it first. Short stories or quick, one-shot novels I won't outline, usually, but major novels and books that are a part of a series I now refuse to start without first drafting that outline.

Question: How do you go about making the geography—the physical world—of a book? (Asked by **Zach Benham**)

This is another answer that's dependent on the story I'm writing. My first two books, for instance, took place (mostly) in areas I was personally familiar with, be it post-apocalyptic Trumann, Arkansas or modern-day Lynn, Arkansas. With both of these stories, 99% of the world was already created for me so there really wasn't much work for me to do in that regard. With the novel I'm working on right now, however, this isn't the case. *Paragon Rising* did present a great challenge for me in this regard. So, I first decided on a name for the kingdom that this fantasy-style story takes place in. I then bought a sketch book and drew up maps for said kingdom. Now, my artistic abilities are—well, they don't exist. I mean, my stick figures look mutilated. Still, this was a much easier process than I'd thought it would be. Once I had the basic map down the rest just fell into place. One reason I love games like *Elder Scrolls V: Skyrim* and *The Legend of Zelda: Ocarina of Time* is your journey takes you across multiple areas, from forests to deserts to mountain tops and ocean-side beaches. I also think of the characters themselves when creating the world they live in. With *Paragon Rising,* for instance, one of my main characters is Gilad Victus, a young boy on the cusp of manhood. He's a hardened survivor of countless marauder raids that his local liege lord doesn't care enough to stop. I really wanted the landscape and geography of his home province, The Vale of Twilight, to match this hardened existence. So I made it a coastal territory with rocky beaches and mountainous terrain that makes life there difficult. So, for me, it depends on the story, its setting, and the characters themselves.

Question: What is your opinion on Fanfictions? Do you support them or do you think they're plagiarism/theft? (Asked by **Anonymous**)

As I alluded to above, I've always been a major supporter of fanfiction. In fact, the first piece of fiction I ever wrote was a fanfiction (It was my version of *The Phantom Menace* written on my mom's typewriter six months before the movie was released). Growing up, I began writing fanfictions and posting them on the website www.fanfiction.net. Here, I'd have other writers and readers fall in love with my stories, but more importantly they'd offer me criticism of what I'd done wrong and some even offered me advice on how to fix it. As I got older, these fanfictions helped me improve my writing style, resulting in better grammar, better spelling, and better stories overall. I would not be where I am today, in terms of my writing, without writing fanfiction. I do understand, of course, where some authors despise fanfictions (the site I mentioned above has a list of authors who've asked them not to allow fanfictions of their materials to be posted on the site, a request, of course, they honor). Some could legally consider it theft of intellectual property. However, these fanfictions are never done for monetary gains (90% of them even have such a disclaimer at the top of the story). My personal opinion is this: if my writing hits home for someone to such a degree that they spend their time writing a fanfiction, a story that expands on my own writing—well, to me that's one of the most flattering compliments I can receive as an author. For me to touch someone's life to that extent makes me feel special and appreciated.

Question: Which author(s) has inspired you the most? (Asked by Danielle Benson)

J.K. Rowling, hands down. Not because the *Harry Potter* series is arguably the best modern work of literature in the annals of humanity, or because those seven books taught me so much about being a decent person, but because of how it all began. I mean, being on welfare, being at ground level—when she wrote Philosopher's Stone (Sorcerer's Stone for my fellow Americans), she wrote it down on a napkin at a local café. She had no guarantee that it'd ever even leave the ground, but she never gave up, she believed in herself, and more importantly she believed in her story. That's a dedication and stubbornness that I've taken to trying to emulate when it comes to my own writing. Equally inspiring is that she's refused to allow the mistakes she's made to define her legacy, and that's something I myself can definitely respect.

Question: Have you ever had sex with someone else's spouse/significant person? Have you been that Other Person? (Asked by **Anonymous**)

Well, that went from 0 to 60 real quick, didn't it? The answer is, of course, Yes. Yes, I have. Twice. Once with my best friend and once with a relative's other half. That's all I'll say—no names, no identifiable markers. All I'll say is both times their boyfriend/husband/significant other had locked them into a relationship in which they were no longer happy, and we began to talk about it, emotions ran high, and, well, as I'm so fond of saying, 2 + 2 = Fish. And, for those who are curious, whether or not this makes me a bad person I don't know, but I don't regret either time.

Question: Why do people—yourself included—hate our President? Why is it so hard to support him and encourage him so that he can be the best President he can be? (Asked by **Damien Long**)

I would first like to explain that I am neither Republican nor Democrat, but rather an Independent. I am one of the biggest opponents of political parties that you shall ever meet. Barack Obama, John McCain, Elizabeth Warren and George W. Bush are four of my most respected public figures.

Obama was a classy leader who, even though I didn't vote for him in 2008, gave me an America I could truly believe in. George W. Bush was a piss-poor President who's only shining moment was keeping us together following 9/11 (I don't think anyone else of that time could have done it better), but as a man—he's a good man and when I see him talking with soldiers *he* sent into battle I can see he genuinely cares for them. Elizabeth Warren has shown us that a woman can be every bit a fearless, effective leader as any man, and John McCain was, perhaps, our last living statesman. Even when you didn't agree with or respect his policies, you respected him as a courageous, classy man.

I say this because I want you to understand that my absolute hatred for Donald J. ~~Twat~~ Trump isn't just about politics. I, and many more like me, despise him so because he glorifies everything that I've been taught for 32 years is Anti-American. Mocking a disabled reporter on live, national television. Stroking his ego on Twitter, demeaning and degrading anyone who opposes him. Asking two foreign nations to investigate a political rival. Using the U.S. government to enrich his own company (from taxpayer money spent for his protection at his own properties to diverting military flights to a small, failing airport in Scotland to keep it afloat so that it, in turn, can help keep one of his nearby failing properties in business. Appointing his children to high-level government positions despite a lack of experience or knowledge for such a volatile position. Winning the presidency despite losing the popular vote by nearly 3 MILLION votes. Denying that the human race is killing our homeworld. These are only the top reasons I despise him. Trump has turned America into global laughingstock. We are at the point where most Americans are safer when going abroad if they hide the fact they're American. Just days before writing these words, I watched as Trump gave the orders for all American forces to withdraw from northern Syria, leaving our Kurdish allies, some of our staunchest supporters in our war on terror and against ISIL, to the mercy of Turkey. And it wasn't even a standard military withdrawal, it was a retreat. Our forces were outbound within 24 hours. We didn't declare victory and bring our troops home, we ran away. What we did to the Kurds in Syria is just as bad as if the French would have suddenly pulled their troops and ships out and went home right after we laid siege to the British at Yorktown. We left a power vacuum that the bad guys will now fill. 11,000+ ISIL prisoners may soon go free *after* admitting that if they escape they want to go after Americans. Not Europeans, as Trump proclaimed, but Americans. I ask all of his supporters one question: how would you have felt if there'd been evidence that

President Obama, in 2012, had asked China or Ukraine to investigate Mitt Romney and then, when Congress opened up an impeachment inquiry as a result, President Obama downright refused to cooperate?

I, and so many like me, hate Trump because he's a fanatical, racist, misogynist, morally-bankrupt, corrupt man-child who's taken for himself the powers of three branches of government, raping the Constitution of the United States in the process. It doesn't matter if 3 people or 300 people are in the room; as far as he's concerned Donald Trump is the smartest, wisest, most-experienced man in the room. The American Presidency can*not* be held by someone who name-calls and refuses to listen to those around him who are smarter, wiser, more experienced, and more knowledgeable about certain situations. America cannot survive a President who cannot admit he's wrong or that he doesn't have an answer and then ask his advisors to give him that answer. Ultimately, I hate Donald Trump both because he's a despicable person and because in his administration I see the death of the nation I so love.

Question: What makes you tick? (Asked by Christina Brame)

Honestly, I'm not quite sure myself. As a person, I always try to be kind, fair, honest, and true to myself. I do strive to do what I believe is right, no matter how difficult it might be. However, I do also have a dark side I can and sometimes do embrace. When people do me wrong I get my pound of flesh, as they say. One of my principles in life is when people hit you, hit them back harder and faster. Whatever they do to you, you return the favor tenfold.

As for getting from day to day—there have been times I've nearly ended it all, where I've stood with my toes off of the edge of that great cliff. Yet, I never do, for one reason or another. I am now at a point in life where I take it a day at a time, and my biggest driver is hope, hope that tomorrow will be better than today and that today's failures will be tomorrow's teachers.

Question: Are you single? (Asked by Rachel Lee)

As of September 28, 2019—I am. As per normal in my life, I put my trust and faith in the wrong person. I genuinely loved her but she didn't quite love me. After costing me my job she then up and moved out, leaving me with two small chicken drumsticks, a bag of rice, and a can of tomato soup (along with unpaid rent) to eat and leaving our *five* cats no food or clean litter. I had to pawn some of my video games just to rectify that situation. Eventually, she came and got the cats, I sold off or trashed 95% of all of my personal belongings and moved home. The first week was one of the darkest periods of my life, but it also showed me the value of smiling and laughter and led to finishing this book I'd spent ten-plus years working on. Oddly enough, however, it's given me hope for the future, and hope for love, rather than hardening my heart and making it grow cold. And, I can promise, I got my pound of flesh in the end. All I can say—Karma can be a stone-cold bitch.

Question: What's the riskiest thing you've ever done? (Asked by Anonymous)

That's a tough one; I've done quite a few things that, looking back, were more than just a little risky. It'd either be masturbating in the middle of my fifth-grade class (a girl sitting opposite of me bent over and her shirt came down and I saw *everything*. *ALMOST* got caught), having sex with my brother-in-law's sister in the middle of a city park at night, or running the kitchen at Cass by myself with just two newbie student cooks one afternoon during dinner rush because everyone else was sick or on vacation. Of course, there was also that afternoon at Cass I got caught hiding a shank in my locker that I'd found under my roommate's bed but hadn't had time to turn in (I found it during the middle of the day, when the dorms were locked up. I'd been given permission to enter and change into a clean uniform after getting cleaning acid on the one I was wearing, so I hid it and decided I'd turn it in that night after shift. Except, you know, surprise locker check!

Question: What's the big deal with *Doctor Who?* (Asked by Tim Duty)

To clarify, *Doctor Who* is a British Science Fiction television series, and one of my three favorite shows ever. And my answer is this: *Doctor Who* has taught me not only how to be a good person but how to reign in my dark side, my anger and my rage—and when to let it go while still in control of it. This show has taught me that sometimes being a coward, being afraid, is the bravest thing a person can do. Most importantly, however, it's reinforced the value that I place on a person's life. In addition, as a history nut it excites me to see great moments in history visited and acknowledged, and I also get excited when the show goes into the future because it shows me one of any number of paths humanity might one day take amongst the stars.

Made in the USA
Columbia, SC
30 April 2023